FableLands

Sammy, Jamila, James

Interrogation Part 2

Samuel Colbran

This is a work of fiction. Names, characters, organisations, places, events and incidents are either products of the author's imagination or are used fictitiously.

Fablelands; Sammy, Jamila, James – Interrogation Part 2

Copyright Samuel Colbran ©2018
All rights reserved.

ISBN: 978-1-92568-05-0-8

No part of this book may be reproduced, or stored in a retrieval system, or transmitted in any form mechanical, photocopying, recording, or otherwise, without express written permission of said author, Samuel Colbran

Published by Samuel Colbran
www.samuelcolbran.com

Assisted publishing with Ocean Reeve Publishing
www.oceanreeve.com

I would like to thank, all my readers, for supporting my creativity.

Samuel Colbran

Sammy: Trickster

FableLands Part Four

1

Sandy beaches, water lapping over your feet as you take a lungful of the sweet salty air. You spy a beautiful woman, just enjoying the sunshine, you catch her eye and smile. She returns it back to you. She positions her towel only five meters away and gives you a quick glance, and she lies down on her towel, soaking up the rays of the sun. This will be a momentous day.

Just thinking what line you can use to impress the lovely woman as you stand up and have a little strut over to her and say… **Ignore it.**

When a large folder slams onto the table snaps you out of your daydream! The last thing you see before your dream leaves is the woman looking straight at you with an angry expression, and you catch a look of a small monkey tail.

You blink to focus on the slender but robust woman standing in front of you. She is nothing like your dream.

Oh yes, the thought occurred to you, *I am in an interrogation room*. Realising that you are in a bare concrete room, with a table and a single chair. There is an itch on your nose. Instinctively you raise your hand to scratch it, or, as you like to call it to piss off Ciro, 'Itch it'.

He is a stickler for proper grammar, but you know he will bite every time.

This time you can't, since there is a massive weight on your arm. As you look down, your whole body is encased in an iron suit, with huge boots that seem to be bolted to the ground. Each joint is stiff and need of oil.

What is happening? "Sam, you are here to answer our questions. If you don't, the suit's temperature will be raised by one degree for each noncompliance."

Who is this woman? You think as you behold her meticulously/fastidiously arranged hair, blank, dead-eyed expression. Eyes that make you feel like they can encase your soul!

She reminds you of that creepy nurse with no sense of humour from that old movie with that actor that played the Joker. You hope the resemblance ends there, as your humour is your best weapon.

"Answer questions?" You said, aiming for roguish. "We have barely met! My name is Sam Wong. Pleased to meet you."

Her monobrow arches. You have seen this look before: Not amused.

"We know your name, boy. We are aware of much of you and your friends. But if you want to be a good boy you can call me Jane Smith."

"Jane?" At just that thought, 'Jane Doe', a feeling of mirth rises in your belly. "Pleased to meet you, Jane. Or should I call you Nurse Ratched?"

Her stare could peel paint off a wall, but, as always, it's like water off a duck's back.

"Either Jane, Ms Smith or Ma'am. For that, we shall give you a taste of what could happen." She looks up to the corner of the room. "Left arm, full."

Like an element on a stove, a lined section of your left arm starts to glow an orange colour. It starts off as unpleasant, but as the colour intensifies, you can feel the flesh of your arm becoming hotter. Sweat beads down your face. When it hits the arm, steam is created. You can feel pressure as well inside the arm, as there is gas that needs to escape.

It moves from unpleasant to outright painfully. You can feel your arm cooking in the metal arm. Gritting your teeth to control, a scream escapes nonetheless.

Jane smiles, and you notice a flicker like a bad video rendering. Must be because of the pain. "Turn it off."

The glow starts to fade, and you hear several small pops as valves open to allow steam to discharge. You don't want to know what that stench is, but it is evident that's how the factories in 'Soylent Green' would smell like.

Putting on a brave face, you casually say, "I have been in hotter saunas!" Her face doesn't even budge, it seems to be made of marble, it's so cold and hard. "Yeah, doesn't want to smile, might break that statuesque face of yours."

Not your best joke, you admit, but you are in pain. You need to stay conscious. *If you let go of the pain, you will have a visitor!* Still, nothing.

How to deal with a humourless person? Or this weighted iron suit. What would your Arc do? Summon his stick and break these bonds and fight his way out of here. Probably piss on someone on his way out.

No point thinking about it now, though. You are no Monkey Magic now. Can't even talk to that buffoon, let alone summon him.

She is just sitting there watching you. Is she even breathing? "Have you heard this one, I tried to catch fog yesterday, I mist. Get it? Mist!"

Your Ratched flips open the folder in front of her and calmly leaves through the pages.

"Okay, okay not my best. I rocked up to school late, my homeroom teacher came out, yelling 'You should've been here at 9!' I replied 'Why? What happened at 9?'"

Not even a twitch. She picks up a page. "If you have finished, shall we begin?"

"Sure, beautiful," you say, hoping that your banter can distract you from all the pain. Next time you see Ciro, you are so going to punch him in the face. *How dare he make such a crappy plan?* You hope he is creating a new one, like 'The Great Escape'. You would be Angus Lennie, and Ciro would be Donald Pleasence. Briana would be Charles Bronson, because of the hairiness.

She apparently didn't find it funny, since rather than interrogated, suddenly your left leg feels like it engulfs in flame. Shaking your head, you look down, and the whole leg case is orange... As you try to hold back a scream, it comes out as a squeak and a hiss.

"Listen to me you, pathetic cow!" you growl, low as a dog. "Turn that off, or else!"

The pain is starting to turn into numbness. That is never a good sign.

She looks at you and smirks, a putrid smile, devoid of humanity. "Was that order you just gave me, now? Maybe we just liquidise your leg and see how you go then?"

"Fine," I hissed through clenched teeth. "Ask your questions."

She looks at the corner again, with a finger swipe across her throat. Your thoughts are not very pure-looking at that action. "So, let us begin."

&r

She clears her throat and shuffles the pages. While this is happening, the pressure is again released from your appendage. Steam flows into the small room.

The smell of Soylent Green fills the room. For one second there you notice, Nurse Ratched sniffing the air, and she looks like you that time after you challenged James to an eating competition at that All-You-Can-Eat taco place.

Never again

Ratched is immobile while taking in the aroma of your roasted parts. Another flicker, as though changing the reel in one of those old movie theatre projectors.

At the edge of your vision, you think you see a tuft of fur. Should know what that looks like, from your experience with your Arc, Sun Wukong.

She finally opens her eyes. For a moment, you feel like prey, and her irises have a slight vertical slit. Strange. "So we want to go over the creation of the Arc Device. From analyse of your household computer, we found traces of calculations on gem growth and power absorption in the synthetic gemstone. What was the size ratio to power absorption for the gemstones?"

"Straight to the point, well, um, x squared plus y squared equals circle."

"Maybe you don't quite understand the question, you have just experienced some discomfort."

"Yeah, a raging burning pain is a little uncomfortable."

"We will let that one slide." Lucky you! You think "Again, and take your time what is the algorithm of your computations?"

"Really, to be honest, I was just the copier. Someone else came up with everything. Sorry, that isn't the answer you wanted but it true."

She again looks again at the corner; this time you notice her left hand is under the table. "We don't want to hurt you, but we know you have knowledge of this."

"Fine, I know I can't out smart you Jane. Copy this down. Got a pencil?"

"Just call it out, and we will record your answer."

You take a deep breath. "Go jump, lady! I am not telling you anything."

She arches her eyebrow at you, raises a hand and smiles. You know what she is going to do.

Think fast, Sammy!

"If you have me, then you have the rest of us. I am just the charm of the group; not the brains."

Ratched sucks in the air through her teeth, smiles at you. There was no warmth in that smile, it is akin to watching a cat play with a dying mouse.

"You are vexing us, Mr Wong. Or do you prefer Sam."

Looking at her smiling make your blood freeze in your veins, or it could be shocking. "Do I have a choice? Call me bitch lips for all I care."

She chuckles at you. "We have chatted with some of your friends, but we know that you were an integral part of the creation of the Arc Device."

What would John McClane do? You ponder, not what he was like in the later movies but when he was hard! Die Hard. Nurse Ratched watches you while you laugh at this.

"Sorry, I was just thinking of a movie."

Suddenly your right leg starts to heat up. The orange glow increases in intensity. Just before it becomes overwhelming again, Ms Smith puts her hand on the table with a small controller. You can see she is holding down the lower right button on the remote.

As the heat reduces on your leg, Jane turns and says to you. "Please what movie was that?"

Your eyes open with incredulity, "You are not serious."

From her face, how little she gives away, you can tell Ratched is dangerous. You swallow. "I was thinking about Die Hard- The first one, not the last one that came out. That was such a stupid movie."

"So, you like being the underdog? John is very much given a no-win situation, but he comes out on top. You might be too young to know this, but no one sees Mr Willis as an action hero as he was too much a funny man. Are you funny-man, Sammy?"

Though you're not sure how to take this, you want to snap back with a retort. Then you notice her finger lightly tapping one of the buttons on the remote. It felt like watching Darth Vader cup his hand. I knew my lack of answers disturbed her. As you mumble the words hoping that she will not push that button. "No, I am not a funny man. Just a kid who loves movies. That is it."

"So, you aren't a master of qigong? With your magic stick, you could break out of here in a jiffy, no? We must be mistaken. We thought you were equal of heaven."

You know that if you were who she was talking about, this room, this facility, and everyone in this place would be dead, including your friends. You start to mumble the song from Monkey Magic again, picturing the actor in his hair and makeup, being stupid and funny.

Born from an egg on a mountain top
The punkiest monkey that ever popped
He knew every magic trick under the sun
To tease the Gods
And everyone and has some fun

Monkey magic, Monkey magic
Monkey magic, Monkey magic

Monkey magic, Monkey....

"What are you singing? The Monkey Magic theme song?" She just laughs at you. "We knew from our research that you love watching Monkey, but do you think he will come and save you in here?"

You shut her out, just whispering the song over and over again. You glimpse something in the corner of your eye. Something furry and cheeky and nurse-killing.

A monkey, just floating there on a pink fluffy cloud, patiently waiting. He holds a little stick and a golden crown on his head with two feathers sticking out of it. His tail wrapped around him, just waiting for your next move

Slamming her fist on the table, she yells at you, brandishing the controller in her other hand. "Don't look at that thing, pay attention to me!"

You still continue to look over at the funny looking monkey, who now is sticking its tongue out at Ratched. "Aren't you a funny little guy?"

As you look back, Ratched's face has turned red with anger, but there is some sort of orange tint with dark shadows mixed in there as well. Like she is taking on tiger stripes.

She picks up a folder and throws it at your imagined monkey, this shocks you as no-one has ever reacted to your Arc's manifestation. Her face is completely gone and what is there is a tiger head but different. Like a demonic version of a great cat's head, on a man's body. He, not she, has their chest exposed with orange fur trailing down the body.

"Listen to me, Mr Wong! You don't see anything in that corner! Just ignore it!"

The tiger-man is gone, and Jane is back yelling at you. Her face is blotted with red spots, and the vein in her forehead is bulging. She yells something that you can't quite hear and points the controller at you.

She then pushes two of the buttons, and your right leg and chest explode into agony. You know that the blackness will take you. The Monkey has grown and is now wearing some robes, and he smiles at you.

Darkness takes over.

Sân

Mist and smoke cloud your eyes. You swipe, and with each movement of your hand, the smoke changes colour. It takes on shades of blue and pink, with some violet and vivid green here or there. The air itself was like a perfume/drug, it was so intoxicating.

Using your hands to navigate through the mist, you feel that you are not in Kansas anymore. Also, that you are not in pain. What is happening to you seems as fleeting as water running through your hands.

The mist parts and you see something very familiar. It is from the TV show Monkey Magic. It is a large area, open to the heavens. On the top of a stair case lies a Jade arc way, In the centre of which is a huge peach tree, lowered with golden peaches. Surrounding this is a huge semi-circle table, with chairs for the Jade Emperor and his heavenly host.

You feel as though you have died and gone to your favourite show, Monkey. It is like walking on the set of episode one, 'Monkey goes wild about heaven.' There are the nine-thousand-year-old peaches where Monkey became immortal in the show.

This must be what your ideal of the FableLands was. Briana sees a castle and knights in armour; Ciro, the pillars of Rome; Jamila, the black and white bright lights of Hollywood, a noir style feel to it.

James has never divulged his ideal FableLands, but it must be fantastic as he grows huge when he becomes one with his Arc.

This is what you want to see, but every time you cross the threshold, your mind is blank to the details.

On each of the plates in front of each chair is a golden peach. You think this must be the Peach of Immortality. As it is a dream, why not have a taste? It would just be an ordinary peach, as you have no idea what they would taste like.

Reaching out, you grab the peach. Your mouth salivates for the chance to eat one of these legendary fruits. Hands are shaking with excitement as you are about to take a huge bite.

The peach is smacked out of your hand by a staff with a gold cap. You turn around and see King Monkey, Great Sage, Equal of Heaven. The yellow scarf, the red shirt, the massive mutton chops, and, upon his brow, is the magical golden headband.

King Monkey is there, flying on his cloud. This has become the best day ever!

He looks at you. "You are not a demon? Where did you come from?"

"Um, my name is Sammy, and I am your number one fan!"

"Wow, really? Fan? Marvellous." He steps off the cloud and slaps you on your back. Pulls a jug from his belt. "Here, let's have a drink with my number one fan!"

You look at the jug, thinking this is all a dream. What could one little sip do? As you bring the flask to your lips, something pops into the corner of your eye. Monkey has a tail!

In the show, Monkey never had a tail. The jug drops from your lips, and you stare.

"What is it, Fan?" Monkey asks, suddenly realising what you are looking at. "Yes, it is my tail. I am the Monkey King! It is the one thing I just can't escape." Picks up his tail and you hear a slight sigh. "Drink up, and pass it back."

Something feels familiar about this scene, but, if this was truly the show's set of Heaven, where is the Heavenly Host? Where are all the Asian actors with poorly dubbed dialogue? And Monkey is speaking perfect English. This doesn't feel right to you.

You hand back the jug. "No, thank you. I can't drink; I am underage. I'm not old enough to drink." That was one of the worst lies you have told in your life. "Um, where am I? This is not my FableLands is it?"

Monkey grabs the jug and then makes it fly like a bullet towards one of the peach trees, too fast for the naked eye to see. "It was the tail, wasn't it?" he growled. "All of my shapeshifting, and I can't hide my tail. Why can't I master those magics?"

As you watch him yell at the heavens, his appearance starts to shift. At first, his red shirt and yellow scarf disappear to be replaced with golden chain mail. His circlet is changed to a circlet of red gold adorned with feathers that seem to burn without catching anything alight. His boots turn into sandals of burnished bronze with stylised clouds etched into it.

His skin starts to grow golden brown hair all over, and his face becomes more monkey-like, less human.

"Who are you?"

Monkey turns and looks at you, his eyes not looking human anymore. Looking at them is like staring at deep pools of eternity. "I am Sun Wukong, Líng-míngdàn-hóu, Shí Hóu, Qítiān Dàshèng or Great Sage, Equal of Heaven. You know me, you have known me for all your life."

He shifts, first into the young lady on the beach, then into your childhood puppy, and one more time to change into the actor Masaaki Sakai. Shimmering back into his 'King' form, he asks, "Which do you prefer? I am everyone and no one."

"You can't be a girl from my dreams," You say, your brain finally catching up to what you have done with that dream girl of yours. "That was you?"

Sun replies. "Yes, I do have to admit being your wet dream was interesting." He pauses and looks you up and down and continues. "I am your first thought as you wake, and when you drift off to your dreams of movies and television, I am there to comfort you."

"You are just a myth, my Arc is Monkey from the show!"

Even as you say that you know that there has always been more, but you have resisted this 'god' for longer than you can remember.

Sun jumps upon the table does a graceful spin, and with one motion he is lying on top of the table with a peach in his hand. "Ah, yes, the show. He is an avatar of mine. A crude avatar, but one nevertheless. As with all the movie renditions that depict me, they are all part of the real Sun Wukong. But you are someone special."

"What do you mean 'special'?"

He raps you on the head with Ruyi Jingu Bang, his golden band staff

You stand there rubbing the lump that is forming because of the bump he gave you. "What do I mean 'special', you know special. One who can hold my true awesomeness!"

From that he starts to bounce around you, chittering and chatting, like a small monkey. Rolling and jumping like he found a stash of his favourite food.

As he finishes, with a blink of an eye, he is next to you with his arm wrapped around your shoulder. "Do you know how boring it is being Dòu-zhànshèng-fó, that sounds much better than…"

"Victorious Fighting Buddha," you said, feeling quite amusing, "I know what it means. According to the legend, you have been granted Buddhahood."

The monkey jumps back on the table, scooping up another peach with his tail. "Yeah, that was fun for maybe a millennium, but I am become bored out of my head. I want to come down the mountain and do a little fighting."

This starts to sink in. The more Sun talks, the more you realise that he isn't talking about being an Arc for a host but indeed manifesting on Earth.

"So, I am special…, so you want to be my Arc."

Knowing it is a redundant question, you need to gauge the real reaction of this entity. "Arc, no." He starts to laugh and bounce around. He just appears again next to you and whispers. "I want to be you."

"What happens if I don't want to be you?"

The Monkey raises his eyebrows at you. "Not like you have a choice, he whispers again, as you realise he's holding you.

A shiver cascades down your spine, as you push off Sun. He just stands there like an unmovable mountain. You then try to get out of his arms and his grip just tightens. "This isn't how an Arc is supposed to work! You are just the embodiment of the archetype we are attuned to."

He looks at you and shakes his head. The fur on his face brushes against your cheek as you hear him take in a huge breath.

"I am SUN WUKONG!" He screams at you, to then resume a seductive whisper. "I am no Arc, boy. They are but mere fractions of the actual powers in

FableLands. Only you have chosen to connect to a God!"

He steps away. Sun picks up his golden banded staff and points to emptiness. "Come! Let me show you what your fate will be should you refuse my gift!"

Sun starts to move the staff's tip into a circle. Faster and Faster. At the end of the staff, a whirling pool of colours cascades into a portal.

He grabs you by the collar and throws you into the swirling mess of colour.

Sì

You blink as you are thrown through the portal, then realises that you are back in the same interrogation room as you were before. There is that metal contraption that they have been torturing you in. As you look, it is currently empty.

Sun steps through the churning pool and starts to laugh. "Welcome back to the real world, Sammy!"

"How did I escape from that?" You ask out loud not to anyone in particular.

Sun Wukong answers you. "You haven't escaped. You sort of died. The Rakshasa pushed your body a little too far, and your heart stopped due to the shock and pain."

"Rakshasa? There was only that woman in here."

He slaps your back of the head. "Foolish boy! You think that it is only your friends' Arcs that live in the Fable? No, no! All the myths and legends live in there."

"So, you mean one day I meet the Hydra?"

He starts to chuckle. "Yes, yes. And much more. You and your friends opened the portal to our realm. Once free, it can be used again. It has been a millennium since the entrance was exposed. And from me to you, thank you."

That chill that started in the other place has not stopped. Now you think it isn't fear, but the touch of death. "But that isn't how Arcs work! There are the three laws!"

He rolls his head back and starts to laugh and laugh. After a few moments, he looks back at you with tears in his eyes. "Rules? Laws? There is nothing like that. It was your friend, Kayla, who bound us to these Laws. That is why she is the scariest of your group. She understands the true nature of the Fable."

"Um.."

He hushes you. "Come let me show you."

He grabs your arm and starts to move towards the door. As you come to the solid door, Sun just puts his arm through it and drags you with him. The sensation of moving through a solid object is weird. You swear you can see the molecules that make up the alloy in the door.

As you come through the other side, guards are marching in unison around men and women in lab coats. The corridor is long, and there is a series of doors up and down each way.

"This is a little annoying," he said, flustered. "Let me show you what is actually happening here."

With a small chant, a rosy tint falls over your eyes. The men and women are the same, but the guards are not human anymore. It is a projection that supersedes the original image, like a film cut using the Schüfftan effect. Most of the guard look like zombies from Dawn of the Dead while some have spines of bone protruding out of their backs. Their eyes are slanted, reptile's, and they are covered with scales. One looked like a Werewolf and another like a Frankenstein's monster.

"What is going on here?" You demand of Sun.

Sun again laughs and moves over to a 'guard' and turns him around. The face is a mess of worms. "See? This one is called The Worm Who Walks, a hive mind of worms that make themselves look like a human. Weird, this one." He spins another around. "This is a Golem. Not the best talker, but will do anything you want as long as you place a little note in his mouth."

He plucks a small scroll out of thin air, along with a pen. He writes something down, opens the guy's mouth and pops in the note. "This will be fun."

The guard pulls his sidearm and points it at the closest person in a lab coat and pulls the trigger. A mess sprays across the opposite wall. Again he turns it to the Wormy guard and pumps three bullets into it. As the body drops, the image of the worms disappears and the only one left is a man in a tactical outfit.

As you are about to ask a question, the guard turns and fires at you. There was no way you could dodge that.

You feel the bullet enter and exit you. The feeling is strange, you look down and nothing.

No blood, or even a bullet hole.

"Why do I feel like a ghost from the Frighteners?"

Sun looks away from the madness he created. "Because you really are not here, this is the Astral. You can't be hurt here, but if your body dies then you go off to the Fable, and I have to wait for another century for another potential host."

That flipness of the Monkey King doesn't sit right with you. "So why are we here? If I am going to die, then this was my time."

"Come. Let's see your body. And then, if you want to let go, I will pave the way for you."

As you walk down the corridor, Sun amuses himself pushing or tripping anyone who shows any sign of being a monster. You move through a scientist but bump into a guard.

"How come can we interact with some people but not others?"

"I thought you were a smart boy. Well, nearly dying can make you a little out of whack. Those 'people'," he points to the overlapped images of monsters. "Are from the Fable. They are those who have not been bonded with a 'monster'.

"These people are pretty stupid. Not control or forethought. Oh, well, let us keep moving so much to see, and you don't have too much time left."

Ignoring the 'not much time left', you grab Sun. "What do you mean bonded to monsters?"

"Okay, I'll tell you. When you went on that field trip to the power station, Ciro wanted to use that power grid to power the Arc device. Can you remember that?"

Your mind floats back to that time. Suddenly, the air around you starts to change. And now you are looking at yourself when you were ten, and you are in your garage with everyone else

"What do you mean we have to break into a power station?" Briana exclaims.

Ciro, with his annoying, arrogant voice. "I need the power to charge this up to full. If I do that, then we can actually connect to this FableLands."

As Jamila enters the conversation, you sit there next to James. He has fixated again with Jamila's ebony face. You think about how she is way out of his league. This is no rom-com where the huge guy gets the attractive girl.

"Please Ciro, we are not idiots. From Sammy's calculations, we do need that sort of power. But, really. Isn't that too dangerous."

"Kayla, I don't have the patience to explain. You do it." Ciro grumbles.

Briana scoffs at Ciro. They always bump heads, but you know deep down inside they really care for each other as friends. And just friends!

Kayla floats to be next to her brother. Even if they look alike, they are like chalk and cheese. "I had a dream last night. It told me that we need to become these Arcs. A great evil is coming to consume the world, and we can only win together. Also, it is within the parameters to not put us in harm's way."

Briana speaks up. "Fine, there is a big evil. But breaking into a Power Station? There must be a better way."

A thought came to you. "What about that upcoming year's field trip for school. If I convince my mum that I want to be an electrical engineer, I can have her 'persuade' our teacher to send us to the local power station."

James smacks you on the back. "That is a fantastic idea, Sammy!"

Rubbing your shoulder, you look at the smiling behemoth. "Thanks, Jimmy, but next time just a light pat. You nearly knocked my shoulder out of its joint, and there is no way I am putting it back in like in Lethal Weapon 2!"

An arm grabs you and pulls you back into reality. "That is enough of that! Oh, want to see something."

Your arm still tingles from James' slap, what is going on here?

Sun grabs your arm, then pulls you through another door and says. "That is it."

He points to the stainless-steel table with a person on top. As your comprehension of the situation hits you. That is, you on that metal slab, your skin is blackened and oozing.

"So, did you want your Sammy, well done or Medium rare?" In his hands, there is a carving knife and a fork. He is now wearing a chef's hat. "And did you want white," he touches your still chest, "or dark?"

With the touching of the leg, you turn and throw up, and the only thing that comes out is ectoplasm.

Wū

I'm *dead,* you think to yourself. That is the cooked corpse of a dead guy. How long did that Rakshasa continue to push the buttons after you died and went to the Fable?

"Pity, you were the perfect avatar for me." The words from Sun seem hollow and distant. "If only there were some way I could save you, hmmm? *Did you* want me to save you?"

"How?"

He reaches behind and grabs that ceramic wine jug from before. "With this, of course." He sloshes the wine, enticing you with its importance. "With a drop of this elixir, you will live. But there is a cost..."

It must mean be he wants to control you. You think you hear at the edge of your hearing. "So what does this cost?"

"Simple. You have to get used to being this age, as you would become immortal."

It dawns on you, that is the Elixir of Immortality.

He will give me that? Your mind goes into overdrive, like in every movie you have seen. This is too easy!

"Doesn't that seem a bit lopsided?"

Don't trust him. "You mortals always see that there must be a catch," he shrugs. "I don't want you to die, you don't want to die. So, it is a win-win scenario."

This is the real world, there is no such thing as a win-win. Your parents know that very well. If you could give up being an Arc to have your parents back, you would do it in a heartbeat.

Then something dawned on you. "If someone died a while ago, would that still work?"

Sun raises his eye brow and ponders on that. "See no reason it couldn't, but it might need a bit more than a drop. This takes me a long time to create. First, the peaches of immortality have to grow, and then I have to make them into wine. That is an interesting process. I have enough for you and maybe one person."

That is going to be hard. Should you bring back you mother or father? Your brain is toxified by that thought. Seeing your mum again. Having her yell at you because you haven't cleaned your room. Wiping dirt off your cheek because you have been playing in the BMX park.

She used to embarrass you so much, but you would give anything to hold her again and have her say that she loves you. But Sun would not just give you the tonic for you mother. You made up your mind to make a deal. Whatever it is, you are willing to pay the price.

"Could you bring back my mother with that?"

Sun grins and does a little dance. This doesn't seem good for you. "Sure, sure but I would need a bit more from you. Your life, I would want your life."

Confused. "What do you mean my life? Aren't you going to save me? And then you want to retake my life?"

"No, that is not what I want. I want you to live, but you would be not quite the same. You would give me the use of your body so I can live again."

This is a bad movie, even the premise is obvious. "We do a time share thing, I have my body one day and you another?"

You know the answer before he spoke it. **He will never give your body back, you will be his forever.** "It is all or nothing. If you want your mum back then, you must freely give your body for my use for all time. What is more important, your freedom or your mum's life? You did say 'anything'."

It has been six years since your mother and father were killed. Still, to this day you blame yourself. It was because of the Arcs that they died. If it weren't for your friends, then you would not be here.

What would he do in my body? Everything you have read about Monkey King is that he is selfish and vain. That on the world would be a disaster. But it is your mum you were talking about…

"I need to think about it, could we bring me back and I will give you my answer soon."

Sun just laughs and laughs. "That is not how it works. Now, if you want to live, your life is mine!

We can take him, Sammy! That voice again, it sounds like your Arc, but Sun is your Arc.

Yes, he is related to me, but he is not your Arc. It is me, Monkey.

Who is this?

He made me this deal an aeon ago. I gave in, hoping for more power, but I never knew he would banish me to the FableLands.

So, you are my Monkey, and he is not?

So you can sometimes think! Just because he has the title doesn't mean he is the only Sun Wukong.

This is a bit of a shock to you. Two Monkeys. Whenever you embraced your Arc, that was the voice you heard, not Sun's.

What should I do?

Allow me to join with you, like always, and we will get that wine and save your mother! Remember, he needs you more than you need him, Sammy.

"I do have an answer. Like they say in the movies: Go and Screw yourself!"

You open yourself up to the usual feeling of your Arc filling every fibre of your soul.

It has always been a partnership, neither dominating over the other. You hold out your hand and feel the coolness of your wishing stick. Your mutton chops start to grow, and you look down, and there are the yellow scarf and red shirt.

"How dare you bring that degenerate before my presence!? *I* am your real Arc! Not that reject from a television show."

See? He is all bluster. He has no power unless you let him. "He has proved himself time and time again. He knew the hurt brought by the loss of my parents. You dress up like my wet dreams!"

"You will give me control, or I will tear your soul to shreds!"

He starts to move toward you with his eyes turning blood red, and his hackles rising.

Stand firm! He has no power here. That is why he wants your body. You chose me for your Arc, not him. And I thank you, Sammy.

You stand there with your stick smashing into the ground like a thumper from Dune. With each strike, Sun flinches, he starts to move forward as you break the ground again

"You can't intimate me!" Sun says lifting his golden band staff.

He will fight us for control, we cannot let him best us. You move forward in with your staff ready to defend. Sun strikes down, faster than you can blink. Only instincts and Monkey help that your gún moves to block his attack. Following up with a twist and strike with your own staff, Sun quickly deflects and then presses the attack.

Back and forth the clashing of the staves like from one of your favourite kung-fu movies, the speed of the exchange is dazzling, your eyes have started to adjust to the speed. Less and less are you relying on Monkey's assistance and you have taken the fight to Sun.

As the tempo of the fight continues to come feel like a mere day in training, moving from low defensive form to a high attack form. Sun mixes it up with Qún Yáng Gùn or Shepard staff routine, and you counter with wǔ hǔ qún yáng gùn or Five Tigers Attack, a Herd of Sheep routine.

You start to get the better of Sun, his strikes have little strength behind them. Again you find a hole in his defence, and you stab him thrice in the chest with a combination of thrust.

He looks at you, his eyes full of pain and Sun says."Please give me control, we can time-share like you suggested."

You slam the pole down one more time and Sun is thrown against the wall as you roar, "Give me the wine and I will let you live!"

Sun looks at me and laughs. "Foolish boy, I will just leave you here, one foot in the grave and one out. In a forever purgatory. I shall shout from heaven. You are only powerful now because you are a true Arc. One day, you will be mine."

With that, he disappears.

Your Arc speaks in your head. **I have to go too, we expended too much energy knocking him back. Call me in a few days, and I will try and explain.**

Feeling the energy leaving your body, you can only think that you are still dead. Moving forward and standing over your body, it saddens that you will be here forever. You should get your sheet, just in like the Frighteners.

You go over and stand vigil over your corpse. It is the way. Hopefully, the others will escape.

Then you hear something, like doors opening and closing. Must be something else. The door opens and in steps Jamila. She must be in full Arc mode, being in her white dress.

She sees the state you are in, and her eyes fill with tears, but her voice sounds muffled, as though listening to someone through a door.

What can she do? She could heal me somewhat if I were living, but that is a corpse.

Her hands start to glow a pink hue, and everywhere she touches the blackened skin peels off, revealing soft, newly healed skin.

Just as you start to fade, your body takes in a breath.

Samuel Colbran
Jamila:Lover
FableLands Part Five

Dangerous Years

The Arcs were caught before they even knew it. James was the first to fall, soon to be followed/ and was soon followed by Briana and Sam. The last thing Jamila felt was a pinprick in the side of her ebony forearm. With a flash of pain, preceded by a numbness that spread from her arm to the rest of her body, Jamila spied Ciro and Kayla dropping and tried reaching out to James before darkness engulfed her.

That was the last thing Jamila noticed before waking up in the predicament that she is in now. The room has a bunk, with a toilet to one side, but the most peculiar thing about it is the buzz from the air ducts, and of course, the floor-to-ceiling glass wall. Beyond the wall are an industrial table and three chairs, leading up to a set of metal stairs that has a glass window with people in hazmat clothes. The faceplates are tinted so Jamila could not see their faces in the suits.

Every so often they come in and attach a plastic bag to a sealed hole, and the sound of a vacuum can be heard as the container is filled with the air Jamila has been breathing.

As the twelfth visitor enters the room, Jamila screams. "Where am I? Let me out!"

She runs over to the wall and bangs on it. There is no sound, as though the glass absorbed the banging, and the hazmat person didn't even look at her.

Jamila is sending out her pheromones to try and find a way to connect with the outside. As she can sense where her pheros have gone, she knows that she is trapped inside this chamber.

Sitting back on the bed, after the last collection of her air, she can sense that a fair amount of her power is in that bag. Closing her eyes, she feels the emotional spectrum that is near the container. There are flashes of crimson to yellow, each aura spike showing Jamila that they are communicating with each other. And after a few minutes, she loses connection with her pheros. Jamila understands that again they have destroyed them.

Once again, her thoughts are with James and where he is. Jamila is confident that there is no way to conventionally hold him, but, seeing this sealed room, it is clear that they have taken each of the Arcs powers into consideration.

Just to touch him again would make her feel safe, but, without her, James can be emotionally manipulated into doing dreadful things.

She needs to worry about her own predicament, but as she presses her mind to a task, it wanders to thoughts of James and the others. Ciro and Kayla are smart, but need tools or materials for their Arcs' potential to bloom; Briana and Sam have physical abilities, but being restrained could hamper them.

Her thoughts are back on her beloved's state; if only her pheros could leave this place and find James.

He is the most physically apt, but Jamila fears for him, for the emotional trauma he could suffer.

She sits back down and concentrates on her own powers. As subtle as they are, they can do a lot. With her mind blank, a vision of someone comes to her foremind, a blonde woman comes into view. Her Arc, Marilyn Monroe.

"Darling, what are you doing?" Marilyn asks.

"Concentrating. If you could help, that would be delightful."

"How can I help? I am dead at the hands of the people I trusted and love!"

Jamila shakes her head. Marilyn will be hard to get back on track. Always talking about the Secret Service poisoning her because of the relationship with Kennedy. History tells a different story: That she took her own life via overdose.

Marilyn's head pops up. "It was no accidental overdose or suicide! I was murdered!"

Jamila opens her eyes, knowing that this is merely a projection of the personality that is a part of her Arc. "Marilyn, I was telling the truth when I said I would discover the truth and expose it to the world. As you can see, however, this is neither the time nor the place.

Marilyn's white skirt flutters, and Jamila notices a camera flash from the corner of her eye. Jamila's Arc goes over and touches the glass. "They understand us, too, don't they? Our powers can't get through an isolated system. What is your plan?"

"There must be a flaw in the system, a gap for my powers to escape. They study the pheros for a while before they destroy them, but those are just small doses. If I concentrate, I could…"

Her Arc holds up her hand. "Pushing and forcing is not who I am, nor even you. You have been listening to Briana too intently. St George is forceful, with his glowing sword; even our lover James is the sexy, muscular type. However…"

Jamila's eyes unfocus/ lose focus as her attention wanders off. She is thinking of James' Arc. She loves James, but his Arc creates an alter ego: Jimy. She knows that Jimy or James will never hurt her, but his power, just like hers, needs to be controlled.

"Yes, yes," Jamila retorts. "We are not. Play to our strengths; be patient."

"See? You are not a dumb girl. But remember that playing the silly girl is one of our strengths, too."

Another reason why she loves James, she thought. He never wants her to play anyone but herself.

But even if she hates doing that, being a beautiful woman has its advantages. Some men are frightened of smart, sexy women, so Jamila has to play dumb to suit the norm.

Her dark ebony skin and mysterious eyes attract men – and some women – to fall into her wiles.

She is, of course, happy to do it if it helps the group, but the cost sometimes seems too high. The unrestrained use of her powers in the past still haunted her.

People can die if they love too much.

Jamila stops concentrating on creating an abundance of pheros and starts to study the body language of the individuals in the hazmat suits.

Marilyn pipes in. "Most of these people are scientists, but the collectors are definitely soldiers of some kind."

"How do you know?" she asks, not understanding how Marilyn came to this conclusion.

"I know army men. They have a stiffness about themselves, but you can feel that potential of action is always bubbling just under the surface. If you could get them on your side, then escape is possible."

Jamila looks at the 'scientists'. "How many women to men?/Male-to-female ratio?"

Marilyn studies for a while. This process is always strange to Jamila, as it is her own perception that her Arc is using, but it makes it quicker to allow her mantle to 'tell' her.

"Out of the ten, there are three women and seven men. Strange, that they overlooked our ability to manipulate men better than females."

"I agree. They must have a reason for this," Jamila ponders. "When will they show their hand?"

The thirteenth collector comes down into the room and again takes out a sample bag. Jamila knows this will be the highest concentration of her pheros so far. One slip up and she can start the process.

Closing her eyes again, Marilyn comes over and places her palms on either side of her temple to help her connect to the pheros. It has gone from feeling to seeing the auras around and how each fluctuates.

As her mind's eye looks around the laboratory, Jamila sees spikes of Blue-Violet showing concertation with light purple and grey. The grey shocks Jamila, as it represents despondency.

Now, seeing the guards, their aura's show bold reds and mixtures of black and yellow streaks. As though they move from being confused to intent/ confusion to intentness. "This seems strange," Marilyn ponders. "If we could only see them without this glass wall. It seems to also block our powers more than we think."

"I can see them clearly outside this glass cage. But, as to the collectors, I don't even get a flash of insight."

The process starts again. Some of Jamila's pheros are taken to another/ a different place.

When they are in a large enough colony can Jamila send her intellect into them, but only to see and feel emotions. The scientists have quarantine standards that are quite high, so beyond seeing auras, there is little she can do.

Marilyn 'shakes' Jamila. "Look! They are staring intently at something."

Correct! Their auras have changed. Jamila cannot see inside the booth, but the flowing colours of emerald green, mixed with light purple, show that they are excited and triumphant.

Jamila opens her eyes, seeing that someone is on the telephone. *Who are they talking to?* She thinks to herself.

"Not sure, but this will lead to either our escape or our staged 'suicide'"

Marilyn is always helpful.

The Asphalt Jungle

While Jamila is looking on, the chief scientist of the Monster Project, Hamill Cornwall, is trying to decide who he should send into the room to combat this captive.

BRCorp wants results, and so far each of these children has given him grief. He looks at his four-guard, each with their minds wiped, tongues removed and control chip inserted. No manipulation of any kind, especially from the Hosts John and Rosemary.

He has already lost subject four, due to monster instability. He needs to look at the data and choose more logical and stable interrogators. Watching the information gathered from each of the subjects' home and family, he concludes that the Succubus is the best against Subject Five.

Pressing down on his intercom. "Janet, send in Rosemary."

"Certainly," Janet replies with a metallic voice.

A soft knock on Hamill's office door, "Enter."

A beautiful woman. A sight that would stir any man's loins, but is amplified by the monster bond. She has dark, auburn hair that falls in heavy curls, sparkling and intense green eyes, and come-hither lips that are plump and red. Hamill looks on and sees a tool, nothing more. He has no attraction to either sex, but even then, Rosemary still flutters his heart ever so lightly.

Hamill motions to the chair. "Sit."

The graceful movement of the Succubus is astonishing, but Hamill can tell she is nervous as all four of his guards have guns in hand, waiting for his signal. Thinking to himself, he reflected that the Succubus' Host would have to be dissected soon to see what genetic changes the monster has done to the model in front of him.

"You will be going into Subject Five's room. Her pheromone levels have spiked, and we can see that she has embraced her Arc. Your mission is to see if your powers can overcome Subject Five's."

"How am I supposed to do that?"

Rosemary's voice is smooth and sweet like honey. She needs to be in a hazmat suit for control reasons. "Simple. We will do this in stages; like all good experiments, controlled steps. The first stage is voice, yours against hers."

Rosemary purrs in anticipation. "My mere honey tongue will be enough for her to be wrapped around my pinkie."

I doubt that your powers are even close, but you are expendable. Hamill thinks to himself. "That is why we start with your voice, but you need control. If you lose it, I will replace you with John!"

Rosemary hisses at the thought of that Rakshasa taking over her prey. Neither her Monster nor herself wants their plaything to be taken away. "I thought he was in your bad books, after killing Subject Four?"

Damn it, she knows about that! After this, we will start over with a new experiment. "Yes, and he is about to interrogate Subject Two but I can swap him for this one instead, and you will return to your room."

'Room' is an understatement. Induced coma for the Monster-hosts. Every Host that rebels are shot and destroyed. She is too aware of the consequences of defying Hamill.

Hamill continues, "After using your Seduction voice, we move on to mixing air. This will be a bit more problematic as Subject Five has fantastic control of the number of pheromones that she produces. This could cause you to be the one being 'charmed'."

"My Host and I will deal with that. If it doesn't have the desired effect, we assume it will come to physical touch. That is when we have most of the power."

Hamill grins. After this interrogation, Rosemary needs to be put down. Hopefully, the information he is collecting will create a more stable monsters' host for application beyond the typical control environment. One of these subjects must be the missing piece for balance and oversight of these entities.

Handing Rosemary her orders, he says, "You are dismissed. Report to chamber twelve and get us that information on Arcing!"

The Succubus stands and blows a kiss at Hamill before seductively walking out of the door. Hamill pulls up each Monster he has shoved into hosts, with the Rakshasa, Succubus, Aswang, Minotaur as his four most stable. He was also using some minor ones like ghouls, worms that walk, Ju-ju zombies and shifters for the mindless soldiers has been working out so far.

I need to stabilise these creatures! Hamill knows this to be true but understanding and making it a reality is a more substantial gap than he expected. If Rosemary controls the manipulator of the subjects, then controlling subjects One and Three will be a possibility.

And then a promotion out of this hell hole!

*   *   *

Rosemary's risqué strutting through the corridor is causing the males and some of the females to become aroused. Their sex is permeating the air. This is causing Rosemary's Succubus to come more to the forefront. Snatching one of the weaker men, she presses him into a room.

"Um, what? Sorry," he mumbles.

"Hush, sweet thing. I just need a little charge up. Just stand there and enjoy."

His body temperature has risen by four degrees as Rosemary presses her body against his, as blood rushes toward his groin area, allowing her to manipulate the scene.

"That is it, my love." She nibbles on his neck and moves to his ear and whispers, "Just let go."

With a moan, he grabs one of her breasts, fumbling like a drunk teenager who knows nothing about how to satisfy a woman. Rosemary grabs his groin and twists, bringing tears immediately to his eyes. The pain is evident.

"Please, it hurts." He pleads with her.

"What, this?" She twists again, he screams in pain only to be muffled by her kissing him. Her Succubus loves the tears of the agonised. "Sorry my love, but in pain can bring more pleasure."

Rosemary kisses her unfortunate victim deeply, his life energy gushing towards her, empowering her senses and abilities. She feels a tap on her shoulder. As Rosemary looks over, she sees it is the barrel of a gun.

Looking down at her half-finished victim, she says, "Next time, love, there'll be no interruptions."

As she leaves with the guard, the weak man sobs to himself.

Rosemary laughs. That just gave her the confidence to deal with the so-called Arc.

Don't be stupid! Marilyn has more power than you think, but we will consume both her and her host. Let me have control in there.

Walking next to Rosemary is a naked woman that looks much like her, but has slits for irises; the whites of her eyes are golden yellow. Two small horns growing out of the demon's forehead. Where her backbone should end there is a thin tail with an arrow point on the end of it, and two leathery wings bursting from her back

Rosemary dislikes her Monster having any influence on her body. There are times – when they feed, or emotions are high – when Rosemary loses the notion of time.

And when she wakes back up, dead people are surrounding her.

"No. I am in control today. I allowed you to feed, now give me your power so I can do my job."

The Demon laughs at Rosemary.

You let me into your body and soul. You are mine now! You have had your fun, and now it is my time to destroy my rival, the Lover!

The Succubus grabs Rosemary and pins her against the wall. To the outside observer, it looks like she has thrown herself against the wall and starts to rise up the wall. The Demon plunges its hand into the chest of Rosemary, while she tries to grasp the arm. Rosemary's hands just move through the entity's forearm.

Slowly pulling out its arm, Rosemary starts to shake and spasm. Her eyes become frantic as she swipes at the arm and head of the Succubus.

You foolish creature! I am of spirit; you cannot grab me. Only one from my realm can. I will rip your soul out, and soon my brother and I will control everything!

The last thing Rosemary sees is a shrivelled husk about the size of a small child. The shell's skin is as black as obsidian and looks as though it is just stretched over a skeleton.

Seeing this, she weeps.

The Demon crushes the neck of the husk, and steps into Rosemary's body.

As Young as You Feel

Jamila has been watching people run around and talking on the phone. Marilyn looks at her, "Maybe we shouldn't have shown that much of our power."

"It is too late for that; we need to get out. I am worried about the others." Which she is, but mostly she is petrified of what is happening to James. "If they send someone in, working together, we cannot lose."

As her Arc ponders on that last comment, a new person walks in, and she is wearing no hazmat suit. The people around her start to salute, and she only hands them a piece of paper.

As Jamila looks upon her, a feeling of fear and anxiety runs up her spine. There is something off about this woman, but she can't see her aura, as the pheros have been destroyed.

The change of mood is evident as Jamila watches this auburn-haired woman strut into the chamber and sit down on the chair in front of the glass wall.

With a flick of her hand, the sound starts to emanate through Jamila's cell. She didn't realise how insulated she was to what she could see.

She spoke in a synthetic voice, akin to the one of someone talking to a fan, "You must be Jamila; my name is Rosemary, and I will be interrogating you today."

Jamila mentally looks over at her Arc, and Marilyn is just standing there, not moving. "What is wrong?"

Marilyn turns and moves closer to Jamila. "You are in great danger here. Don't talk to this woman!"

Jamila has never seen her Arc react to anyone like this. The one time she'd seen her like this, it was while watching a sexual predator on television. "What do you mean? I know I am in danger."

"Not like this," she explains. "She isn't human anymore. I need to join you. Otherwise, you are dead, and I will be banished."

Again, with the screech of an overhead communication system. "Is everything alright, Jamila? You look a little drawn."

As Marilyn walks up and steps into Jamila's body, a brief flashback of her Arc's life plays before her eyes. This is a usual thing for Jamila, seeing Marilyn from birth to her murder.

It is disturbing, but a part of the Arc process. For a split second, they are surrounded by flashing cameras, and their white dress springs up with a gust of air from below.

I am here, look at what she is. Jamila opens herself up to her aura sight, and there seems to be nothing alive on that other side of the glass. Something about that transparent wall which is causing her sight to be lessened.

I can't see anything, Marilyn.

She is something wrong, trust me on that. I will protect you from that monster.

"Miss Mirona, can you answer a couple of questions? They are concerning the incident at the power station."

That metallic voice sounds wrong. They want to keep Jamila's influence down.

Don't worry about what happened back then, you didn't understand how powerful your abilities can become.

Jamila knew this, but it didn't detract from the guilt. "Yes, it was a regular field trip while I was in primary school. I think I have been to a station at least four times."

Excellent work, my host.

"Don't play games with me. The one seven years ago, where you and your friends were a cause of the huge blackout of 2013."

This time her voice was smooth like honey, not harsh like a file over a pipe. The words just dripped off her tongue. It was ecstasy. *Just listen to her voice, let it make you forget everything. Her form is everything.*

Shake it off, I am here. "We had nothing to do with that blackout."

"Are you sure? Have I said you are a lovely-looking girl? Pity we are on different sides, as I think we could be very friendly with each other."

"Is that a question?"

"No, just a statement. I miss having women and girls as friends. You have to understand that I miss the old days." She stares a little longer, just enough to make her uncomfortable. "So, we know what happened at the power plant, as the evidence was quite easy to find. I just have to ask, why did you kill that guard?'

Those words hit Jamila like a ton of bricks. Those deaths still weigh on her.

Ciro and Kayla turn to the group with the idea that could solve their power issues. As the team is visiting Wivenhoe Power station, that output could quickly open a stable connection to the parallel world.

"Why do we have to do this, Kayla?" Jamila demands.

Briana was in the hospital for two weeks from the burns of their last experiments. Jamila didn't understand why everyone still wants to go through this.

Kayla again is ignoring Jamila's question because she has become fascinated with the movement of the smoke floating in the air due to the back burning.

Ciro looks up from his latest device. "It is simple. Kayla thinks we are going to need these powers. I don't believe in predicting the future, but her reasoning is sound."

"You only care to see your precious theory being proven right. Well, you can count Briana and me out. We will have nothing of this!"

James places his massive hand on Jamila's shoulder, and, as she turns, his face flushes red. "Um, come on Jamila. I do this time, and nothing can hurt me. I am too big."

As James smiles at Jamila, she shakes her head. His smile is too cute.

"I want to hear the reason again. Tell us now, Kayla!"

Kayla snaps out of her daydream. Partly because Jamila is yelling at her, but mainly because Ciro is shaking her shoulder trying to get her attention.

"Well, I have seen the patterns of this world. Every year, ice caps melt, a new terrorist group pops up every other week, massive climate shifts in parts of the world, causing severe weather from droughts to bushfires to substantial tropical storms. Violence and horror are increasing at an expositional rate, and the world is controlled by the one percent.

"This world needs hope. It needs new heroes. Look back in the myths and legends: some of the Chosen stand up and save the people. We need this, the world needs this."

"I remember that field trip," Jamila said, back in reality. "It was unfortunate that there was a blackout and a guard was killed due to the electrical surge from the turbines. Lucky none of my classmates were hurt."

"Is that really true? I can't say what happened inside, since, for some reason, all the cameras were disabled. But the outside cameras show evidence of injury. Most of your clothes were burnt and ripped, yet there were no wounds or burns on you. Peculiar."

Jamila doesn't answer this. The more she says, the more likely they are to come to the realisation of what happened.

Rosemary clicks her nails on the table. "No response to that. One second; we have something for you to look at."

She stands up and walks into the room above. *What is this all about, Marilyn?*

Not sure, but they cannot be trusted. That creature that you are talking to is wrong.

What is wrong with it? I can't sense anything in here, the glass must be lined with lead.

I am as blind as you to her aura, but it is more her eyes that make me wary. Maybe we should play dumb, like when I dealt with movie producers.

I think that would be a better plan than just being trapped into a banter-off.

Rosemary comes back into the room with a box, she pours the contents onto the table, and it is something that she recognises very well.

It is Ciro's prototype Arc Device.

Don't Bother to Knock

As Jamila stares at the spilt contents of the box, there's a whirring noise, like fans starting. She looks over at the collection area and sees that the fan has begun.

She thinks to herself, *Right, I can start to do-*

As that thought comes in, she notices an essence of a mixture of light and dark pink, with flashes of light purple.

What is the strangest thing about It? Is it the black, smoke-like streak in the lustful cloud? Jamila hasn't seen an unrestrained use of aura for a long time. She concentrates and increases her own pheros around her skin and body to act as a buffer against this unwanted invasion.

The aura of this so-called human is probing around Jamila's defences. It feels like a hot, sweaty hand pressing up against her body, taking her all not to scream.

"Are you alright? You seem a little uncomfortable. But back to the questions."

Now Jamila understands what her Arc was feeling. Overlapping this poor woman's form is a demonic presence. It is sickening that every pore of hers is filled with this unrestrained lust.

Slowly swallowing the bile, she responds with a shaky voice. "I am fine."

Rosemary can see that her influence is in full swing, she just needs to force this Arc to start revealing the secrets. "Well my lovely, you just need to give in and tell Rosemary the truth. What actually happened at the power station?"

Rosemary sends another dose of her spores into the room. She can see them probing and prod her defences. *Just need to force my essence into Jamila, and it is all over. Resistance is like a sweet wine, best to be savoured.*

"There was a fault with ou… I mean the system. This caused the death of the security guard."

Licking her lips, the Succubus is becoming aroused by this defiance. When will stage three happen, physical contact? That mere thought sends waves of electricity towards her pleasure centres.

"So, the explosion and death had nothing to do with this broken device?" She purrs, sending another wave of the blackest passion spurred on by the creature's demonic soul. "Come on, you can tell me, beautiful. Let go, and we can relax."

The essence of the Succubus is penetrating Jamila's pores. Even at this distance, her surface temperature has risen, and her pupils have dilated.

Rose-Succubus cannot hold herself back; she needs to take both of their souls. That would feed her for eternity.

In a dreamy voice, Jamila responds, "Yes, we were the reason for the outage, and I killed the security guard."

Rose is taken aback by this. She was hoping to lure this out of her. Not to have her just succumb to some of her essences.

How boring! Maybe making her relive that could give Rose the pleasure she is looking for.

"Your friends did cause that explosion. So, what is this?"

"It is what Ciro and Kayla call an Arc device. It is to link someone to their counterpart in the FableLands."

Her bosses will reward her with a day pass. What she could do in Sydney! There are nearly eight million tasty morsels in that city. In one day, she will have slaves and food for many years to come. Even enough people to stop them bringing her back.

"Arc Device. Do you know how it works?"

Jamila is waving her hand in front of her face. Rose forgets that her scent can cause hallucinations. Time to pull back some of my principles. The swirl of colours moves away from Jamila, and back through the air vent.

Seeing that Jamila has regained some of her wits, she continues. "How does the device work?"

Owlishly, Jamila blinks at the Succubus. "Um, you need energy. Grown crystals of high quality, and then need to channel that energy into the crystals to open the portal. A substation output is too small for a proper connection. We needed it pure from the source."

This is going better than Rose thought it would. Soon, she would have freedom from these humans, and she will gain the power to bring more of her kind into this world!

"There was a field trip to a power station, how lucky you were."

"Luck had nothing to do with it. After Kayla convinced me of her prophecy, I manipulated the teacher into going to the power plant."

Prophecy. The drones under her control behind her will not give any of this information to Hamill. This company has no idea what they have, let alone how to control it.

"What is this prophecy?"

"Something that hasn't come true. Something about monsters returning, and that we have to become heroes to stop."

After this conversation, the Succubus is going to have a chat with Kayla. She saw their return years before it started to happen.

"Monsters," she reflected. "Interesting. Now, back to the power station. Wouldn't it be dangerous to be in proximity to that vast amount of power?"

"Ciro designed into the device a grounding point to syphon off excess energy that wasn't absorbed by the crystals, and he created a backup just in case, for safety. He learned a lot from his mistake at the substation."

"Interesting. Was someone injured?"

Jamila looks at the Succubus. For a moment, Rose thinks that she sees that her eyes are completely clear, but they sink back into a dreamy-like stare. "Only my friend, Briana. She has severe burns on her face and neck. After agreeing with Kayla, I demanded that Ciro make it safer."

"Did Ciro make it safer?"

"From what he said, the device was much more reliable, hence why we are all here. But he didn't realise the backlash of the connection to the FableLands."

Rose is looking at her victim, just waiting to get her hands on this girl. If she pins her down, she can drain the life not only of the host but the Arc as well.

"According to the records, the 'backlash' caused a system failure that became one of the significant blackouts in the last twenty years."

Again, Rose has noticed that Jamila slipped into a catatonic state. For someone with a similar power-set to hers, Jamila is quite susceptible to manipulation.

The Succubus side doesn't want to pull back, but without some resistance, the physical touch stage will not happen. Changing up her usual tactic, Rose decides that her aggression would be the best emotion to manipulate here.

Rose sits there, wondering how to cause the next stage. This Jamila seems to be connected with another called Briana. She wonders if there is another video she can use to push that aggression.

The aura hasn't affected Jamila. "Questions will start again. Just need to check on something."

Rose seems to hear a mumble as she leaves the room through the door and into the control section. "So what can we use on her?"

As protocol dictates, only women can be on staff against the Lover Arc. The head scientist, Katherine, turns in her hazmat suit. "Why do we need anything else? You have proven to be stronger than this girl, and we have learned a great deal from her."

"I am feeling some resistance to my probing. This compliance will stop very soon, and this girl will move to an aggressive stance, then refuse to answer any more questions. I know what will happen."

Katherine pauses and looks at the data that has been collected. "Her pheromone levels are insignificant compared to twenty minutes ago. Your own aura has either destroyed or smothered Jamila's powers. There is no need for stage three, as you are in control now."

This is frustrating, explaining to this coat why she needs that contact. "I am telling you that she has been pushing against me for that entire time. I need to step it up to the physical."

"What proof can you give us?"

"If she is completely under my control, then an emotional outburst would be a no-go. What is happening with the other subjects? Who is being hurt?"

"You have heard Subject Four was killed by John. Foolish that he allowed being baited."

"Yeah, I talked to John. He thought that putting on Nurse Ratched would freak out the little monkey."

"Our information on subject four's movie obsession was accurate, but he was too aggressive. And now John is dealing with Subject Two, with more restraint on his powers."

"Subject Three's interrogation is about to start, but an expendable grunt will begin his questioning, with Aswang Asylsa as back up."

"Not the best matchup, given that subjects One and Three have all the information. Is that right?"

Katherine looks off in a random direction. "I suggested you be the interrogator with Subject Three, but Chief Cornwall decided to pit your powers against the similar set in the Arc group."

Rose looks out the viewing window. She can see that Subject Five has started to pace, a good indication that the aggression formula is working. "What about subject six, the big lad?"

"As he is just the muscle, our more physical host will see his breaking point."

This could be of use. "Could I get pictures of subjects Four and Six. This will prove whether Five is under my control."

"Give us a moment to set up a stream of the cameras. That QLED television will be wheeled in so you can show it to your subject."

"Good."

This is perfect! Live feed of our torture. And, with my aggression sensation, Subject Five will go crazy!

How to Marry a Millionaire

Marilyn has been keeping this evil miasma away from Jamila, but its potency is staggering, nearly as overwhelming as her own powers.

One thing, though, is that their abilities are more subtle than forceful. You don't need a sledgehammer to push a needle through the cloth, just a deft hand.

Even if most of the evil is pressed back, Jamila is still having an issue: wanting to know what this monster's next step is. The waves of this manipulation aura have taken its toll, but show an insight into a Succubus head. Too aggressive, and she is dying to touch her. Jamila can tell that from the body language; the subconscious clenching of her hands; the heavy breathing when Jamila shows weakness. The strangest of all is the salivating. That has weirded out Jamila a lot, making her feel like some prize steak.

Thinking about her Arc. When shall we take control?

Soon, Darling. This monster was very much like you in the beginning. All force, no skill. But you did learn.

Praise from her Arc is a strange thing. Marilyn always wants perfection. In the way, she walks, how Jamila talks, and how she seduces. Men are easy to manipulate; a beautiful face and sexy body will have most men in the palm of her hand. Except for James, one reason why Jamila loves James. He just does delightful things because he loves to do wonderful things.

Again, she is thinking of him, Jamila will see her James soon and will save him; or him, her.

Jamila sees them wheel in a big-screen TV, wondering what they need that for.

The Succubus comes back in and sits back down, starts again to push out waves of a different aura composition. More deep reds and oranges with streaks of black.

She has changed tactics. Why send that sort of level of aggression and hate? There is nothing to gain with this. Keep your wits about yourself, Jamila.

Rose clears her throat, "I have something to show you, Jamila."

The demon turns on the screen, where James is hanging from his ankles and is then repeatedly anchored to the ground with some strange rope. They have stretched him to the full extent of his body. There is no way he could pull and break his way out of there.

But that wasn't the troubling part.

"Can you see, Jamila? We know he is the brawn of your group, so instead of asking questions, we have seen how far his endurance can be pushed. Here, watch."

Rose doesn't understand even if Jamila was in the real dreamy state. Seeing the love of her life being hurt like this would put her into a rage that would shake the heavens.

A large man comes into view. He has a weird double image. One of a very muscular man and the other is a massive, hairy individual with a bull's head and large horns. In his fist is a length of chain.

Lifting his arm, he sends the chain against James's body, tearing at his clothes, causing welts to appear and blood to flow. James just takes it with a grunt. The bull-man raises his chain high again and hits the opposite side of James, making sure he digs in the chain, so it will cause more pain as he pulls it back out.

Jamila turns her head not to watch. You need to keep watching. This isn't affecting you, as you are under that beast's control.

I can't just watch. This is James!

You will, or we are all dead!

Jamila changes her expression to one of a dream-like a state. "Pretty pictures, who is that?"

Rose-Succubus squints her eyes at Jamila. This girl shouldn't be in a dreamy state. There should be signs of aggression. What is happening here? No, I can't have lost control, she thinks to herself.

Maybe seeing Subject Four being slowly roasted and killed will turn this towards what I want.

"Jamila, I have another lovely picture."

"Ooo, what is it?" I can't do this, it's too hard! This is going to be worse than my James being tortured.

We nearly are there, we just have to spread the influence a bit further, and you can save James. Pretend! You have to do this for everyone else.

Rose makes a signal to the control box, and the screen changes, showing Sammy encased in a massive armour suit. The 'woman' that is in the same room looks like a human with a tiger's head.

They are talking to each other. The tiger-man pulls out a remote and points it at Sammy. The whole suit starts to glow, and the pain on Sammy's face is evident. Something is happening here. The ruddiness increases in intensity and the screaming increases as well, until the scream turns into a croak. The light looks like what you would see on an electric stove.

Jamila's mind rebels as they throw water on the suit and steam hisses off it. The outfit that Sammy was in must have been an oven, and he doesn't seem to be moving anymore.

A growl escapes Jamila's throat. Calm yourself. There might still be time to save him if you are calm.

"Are you alright, Subject Five?" Jamila could see the gloating of the demon. She is getting off on the sadistic feeling caused by her reaction.

Jamila thinks to herself that is enough.

She loses control. She grabs entirely on to the power of the Lover and throws out the power without restraint.

It has been years since this happened. Last time, a security guard killed himself because of the 'love' he had for Jamila.

The Succubus didn't react in time to put up any defences. The emotional attack from Jamila hits Rose like a category five storm.

Rose is completely overwhelmed in a matter of seconds. She is riding the anger and sadness like a leaf in the wind.

"Open the door!" Jamila demands.

Rose stands and walks over like a marionette. She is trying to resist, but her body is just doing as it is being commanded.

Jamila steps through the open door, casually touching the demon lady. A flash of imaginary cameras wipe the mind of this person, and they are now one hundred percent Jamila's slave.

As the door opens above, three guards burst from the control room pointing guns at them both. They all sweep their hands, and their aura of control spins out towards the three guards.

"Turn around and kill everyone in there. To protect me, my loves."

Two of the guards open the control room, showering it with bullets. The wet slaps of bullets hitting bodies sound outside.

Jamila turns to Rose. "You will always stand in front of me because I will reward you with my love."

"Yes, Mistress. And I love you, too."

As Rose says this, the three other guards parrot the same statement. Jamila's rush at the acceptance from these four drives her mad with pleasure, the reason why her power is such an intoxication.

Come back to me. Don't lose yourself, Jamila!

Do you see what they have done to my friends!? They deserve to die a horrible death!

Oh, you are just like the rest! You listen to me while the wine flows and the skirts flutter. But when it truly counts, you kick me to the curve. Very well, then. Be happy with your demon! You've already got my essence

Jamila ignoring the harpy voice of her Arc. She moves through the control room, dead and dying are everywhere. Jamila has no care for what has been done. All she wants is to find James!

Jamila notices a blinking light. "What is that, darling?"

One of the guards says. "It is the alarm of your escape."

"Could you be a dear and turn that off? And Rose, could you tell them it was a slip of the hand. No need to worry."

In unison, they both answer, "Yes, Mistress."

As Jamila hears this, shivers of pleasure every time they say that. After freeing James, we are going to take over this whole base, and everyone will be under my control!

Jamila, this isn't you. Don't give in to the darker side of the control. This is a rabbit hole you can't just jump out of.

Shut up! If it were up to you, we would be in that room watching our friends being abused and tortured. This is the real me, with everyone licking my feet. Now shut up!

Fine, I thought you were stronger. I will be here for the aftermath.

With that, the presence of Marilyn's connection slips into the subconscious of Jamila. "Good! I am free of her." She points at the three guards. "You will protect me and take me to my James!"

They stand there dumbfounded. Rose pipes in. "Subject Six, she wants to find Subject Six."

They leave to control room with two of the guards in front and the other protecting the rear. "Rose, what was the purpose of trying to control me?"

"I am sorry, Mistress. It was not my choice to control you, but we wanted to see if you, the strongest, could be monitored. If that was true, then I was tasked to manage and rip the information about Arcs out of your friends." Rose heads to a wall and starts to bang her head against it. "I am so sorry, Mistress, to ever think like that."

"Stop, you are no good to be injured," she says, then her tone grows darker. "But we will be having a chat about it later."

As several armed people come around the corner, the charmed guards open fire while the third pushes Jamila out of the way.

Every guard they send takes a hit, but they make sure that the Hallway remains covered. With every guard that drops, another takes its place.

After one of Jamila's charmed guards falls, another pulls back to fire from cover. Jamila can see that this one is injured, with bullet holes in the legs and arms.

Jamila says to herself. "Enough of this. Do your duty and attack!"

In unison, the two guards say, "Yes, my Mistress." And they charge down the hallway guns blazing.

Jamila turns to Rose. "You will use your powers down there and command them to run amok in the facility. Then return and show me where James is."

"Your will be done, Mistress."

As Rose turns the corner, Jamila drops. Her ebony skin is slick with sweat and blood. Bile is rising, as she can smell the copperiness of blood in the air.

She has pushed herself too far. She knows that she is sending people to their deaths, and making the demon do it for her doesn't distract from her callous approach to this situation.

She can see the expansion of Rose's aura and scent. It is strange seeing it from this side. Her power is similar to her own but is missing something. After hearing some more screams, the gunfire seems to be moving away from Jamila.

Rose steps back into Jamila's corridor and grabs Jamila. Her true form has overlapped the human shell she has been in. Long black hair with two blood red horns growing from the forehead. Her feet are now hooves, and she has sprouted two leathery wings from her back. The black eyes with the red slits and the razor teeth finish off the package. The smell of sulphur and brimstone is in the air.

"You thought you could control me, little girl. What I have in store for you will make the angels weep." She runs one talon down the cheek of Jamila. "Your mistake was allowing me to use my power to the fullest. Didn't realise the restraint this world had on my abilities."

Marilyn! Please help me.

"Pleading to your Arc won't help you. You are my plaything, and you just told me what will hurt you the most."

The Prince and the Showgirl

Grabbing Jamila by the arm, she pulled her down the hallway. There are people thrown against the wall, bloody and filled with holes. "See? This is what you did! You might even become like me. Just need that little push."

Trembling at the sight of this wanton violence, the blame is apparently at her feet. *I plead with you, my Arc! What should I do?*

As they turn another corner, a set of three guards run towards them with a bead on the two. "Hail and identify!"

"Begone, mortals!"

They aim their weapons at Rosemary. "You have to the count of..."

"Enough!" Rose throws a black and crimson aura down the corridor. The malice and control emanating from it. The mere thought of it makes Jamila bring bile into her mouth. This is what she is becoming, a demon with no morals or control.

They drop their barrels to the ground. Each of them then drop to a knee and say in unison, "Mistress, command us."

"Guard us, kill anyone who approaches." Even in her demonic form, Rose gives off this lure of lust and passion. Men would tear their own skins off to be close to her. "See, my apprentice? So easy. All you have to do is not care. Come. Let us find your boyfriend."

Tears stream down her face, and she does not notice the bullets raging from the echoes. Jamila's only thoughts are that she is lost, and this is her new path. *Please my Arc, I am sorry. Come back!*

The guards have pinned someone against a wall, a sighted(?) man in a lab coat.

Jamila has been lost in her own feelings to see what the state of the hall is now. Blood covers the walls like wet paint; the smell of death and faeces permeates throughout this confined space, and all she can taste is fear and lust from Rosemary.

"Come! It is your turn. Give in, take this man's mind and soul. It is easy, just let go and reach out."

Trembling, Jamila reaches out her hand. Her eyes see into the aura. Fear and anxiety are like a blur of colours, each shouting at her to help, but Jamila just sends her pheros to invade his mind with pure devotion to her captor.

Jamila sees every reaction like it is in slow motion. The hairs on his arms stand on end, his pupils dilate, and she can hear his breathing become akin to that of a panting dog. His heartbeat is rapidly rising to a near heart attack.

Rosemary does a slow clap. "That is impressive. You can smell his devotion. Well done, my apprentice." She touches one of the guard's arms. The reaction in an atmosphere of pure pleasure erupts from him. "Kill him, my dear one."

Before Jamila could react, the guard empties his entire clip into the poor man. His face was first to go, and the last thing Jamila saw was the pure devotion, as his eyes never left her face.

"Why did you do that, I had him under my control!"

"Don't worry, there are more, and much stronger and virile than that weakling. He was merely a test, which you passed with flying colours. We will be doing some naughty things! Your boyfriend isn't far, and he will be your final test."

The shoulders slump and Jamila follows the skipping Demon, who laughs and spits on the recently dead man. *My Arc, how did I come to this? I should have listened to you. Please, do not leave me. I feel that I am slipping into a demon. I am not strong enough. That look he gave me was beautiful. I want to see it again and again.*

Minutes or seconds pass. The only thoughts on Jamila's mind are either sickness at what she did or wanting to do it again. Seeing another man or woman under her control would be ecstatic.

"My apprentice, we are here!"

Rosemary opens a door. The bull-man from before is pounding on an upside-down James. His clothes are strips falling down onto the floor, his body is a mass of bruises and blood. Only one of his eyes is open, and with it he sees Jamila. A grin appears on his swollen face.

The Bull-Man turns and grunts at the Demon. "What you doin' 'ere!"

"Come now, Minny. Just here to create a new monster. Leave this sack of meat to us. We will make him squeal!"

A low chuckle comes from the Bull-Man. "If you do, record it. Been workin' on 'im for ages now. Not a peep! Bloody 'Ero!"

He spits on James and laughs as he leaves. "This be good to watch! But I hungry!"

As the door closes, all that is left is one guard, Rose, Jamila and James. "Stupid cow! But he does have his uses." She points at James. "Now, for your final test."

Jamila looks dumbfounded at James; his stupid grin is still there. He tries to say something, but only a spasm of coughing happens, and blood gushes out his mouth and down his forehead.

"Now my apprentice, the last test is simple. To see if you have really let go and want to step on the other side, you need to watch me kill him. Your love. So sweet, but a waste of time."

Jamila sharply looks at Rose, the rage boiling inside of her. "Tut, tut. If you fail, then you both die… slowly. You first."

A gun barrel presses up against Jamila's head. She freezes. Looking at James, tears start to fall.

Seeing the gun against Jamila's head, his grin changes into a snarl, and he starts to buck against the carbon nanotubes. He starts to wrench his arms up towards his legs at the same time moving his knees to his chest.

"Enough, foolish man. Those restraints can comfortably hold 6 tons each." She fashions a knife from her aura, made from a mixture of red and black, aggression and malice. "I will show you how to do this later."

"Stop this," Jamila pleads to Rose. "I can control him. There is no reason to kill him."

"I guess punishment is in order," Rose sighs. "Shoot her knee out."

The guard moves his gun down to Jamila's knee. Her hand shoots out before she realises it. **"Point the weapon at the Demon!"**

A flash of cameras goes off. Jamila looks down, and she briefly sees a white dress that seems to want to fly up from an imaginary street vent.

"No, point your gun at her!" Rosemary sends out her power, and it hits a wall made from camera flashes.

"No, you have no power here, Demon!"

"You think your Arc can save you? You are like me. Give in, Jamila."

Jamila takes a step forward. This is her path now.

In her mind, Marilyn called out to her. **No, it isn't. Your path is more than lust and pleasure. The Lover is mother, daughter, grandmother. From the first kiss to the last, of your husband of**

many years. She is just the moment, you are love's journey.

"If you don't, I will kill your James." She sends another cascading wave of pleasure and lust at the guard. It suddenly breaks through. "Kill that witch!"

A massive crack can be heard in the room. Jamila seems to be staring behind Rosemary. "Give in, Demon!"

She looks at the guard, and sends compassion and hope towards him. "You are free."

The guard drops his gun, stares behind Rosemary and runs screaming from the room. "Your man is still trapped!"

She spins around with her knife poised to strike.

Jamila says. "Have you meet my boyfriend, Jimy?"

Before her is a massive, nine-foot muscular man, with Samoan tribal tattoos across his vast tanned chest and arms. His wounds are healing as he shakes off the tubes.

Rosemary was right. Jimy might not be able to break the nanotubes, but the concrete is not as sturdy.

"You leave Jimy girl alone!"

The last thing Rosemary sees is a massive fist descending toward her face.

Samuel Colbran

James: Giant

FableLands Part Six

Grey

Being tied to the ceiling by my ankles and strung tight to the ground by my wrists is not my idea of fun. I feel like one of my older brother's guitar strings. What do they think I am, a monster due to my size? I am nothing like my best friend, Jimy.

I told Ciro this was a bad idea. Well, Jimy said to me of his bad feeling about all of this, and see where it has gotten us. Captured! I am in a room with someone who gives me the creeps, looking at me like I am some sort of toy.

For the last three hours, he's pounded on me. I can take the punches and the insults. As long as this brute is in here with me, he is not with the rest of my friends.

All I can think of is why is this always happening to me? But then, people still shy away from me because of my size. People look at me and see a huge man, possibly a stupid and violent man, not the gentle, caring person I really am.

Have you ever been frightened of hurting anyone by accident? Or knocking over someone, because for a split second you weren't watching where you were going? Been there done that, so I don't lift my fist in anger, even when I should have. Only Jimy does that now.

"… and pay attention, stupid!" yelled the man in denim overalls. No shirt but a lot of tattoos. Some of them are interesting; the Hulk one looks fantastic. That is Jimy and mine's favourite comic.

Oh yes, we were captured. And now this brown-headed brute is bashing me. I think because Mike likes it.

I told Ciro that this did not feel like a good plan, and he asked me why in that slightly arrogant way. Jimy told me. A gut feeling, too much danger. Ciro, bless him, can be a bit of a handful, but he should have listened to Jimy.

I watch as the thug comes at me with a bat this time. All I can see in his puddle-brown eyes is bloodlust. "Goin' to scream, stupid?"

Another solid hit, the bat hitting my thigh, not that hard.

My Dad would never scream out he was too strong. I know this because My Dad died when I was five, from protecting us kids from a robber. We were down the street, and he was buying ice cream for us. Then this funny looking man came in, the killer had sores and rotten teeth. He pointed a gun at Henry, the shop owner, and Dad tried to talk him down, so he turned and shot at us kids. Dad is a superhero, so, like Captain America, he jumped in the way and then took the evil man out.

If my dad could handle the evil man, I can deal with this one

"Enough, Mike, give him twenty minutes. The others are not prepped to use the camera work, yet." The voice comes from the ceiling.

"Fuckin' Hamill, takin' away all me fun." He comes over and leans down to pat me on the cheek. I growl at him and snap my jaws to bite his finger off, but this Mike person punches me in the face, stopping me and making my cheek bleed.

Wonder why he wanted those tattoos on his knuckles. Hate. Love. They call me dumb.

"Fuckin' stupid ta try an' bite me. Lucky fer you that Mr Hamill is really borin'!"

As Mike leaves, the door screeching as he exits, I have some time to try and talk to Jimy. Mike doesn't ask me questions, just hits me. Every so often, someone overhead calls him off, and I can relax… well, I get to not be punched or beaten for a bit.

Usually, when I am by myself, I can talk to Jimy, but in here it is strange, he's just not right here with me. Enough to help me not die but not enough to help me get out of here.

I don't have to think not to yell out right now. I can use a bit of leftover Jimy to stop the pain and bleeding.

So, meeting my new family for the first time was when I was jumped by those little thugs. I stopped Jimy from hurting them, I could take it but then came Ciro, Sammy, Kayla, Briana and the lovely Jamila to save me. Now I had friends, and they were smart too.

If they treat anyone else like me, I will kill them, with Jimy or no Jimy. They won't, though; I'm the useless one. I didn't come up with the idea of FableLands, like Kayla or Ciro, or help make the device. I'm not a great leader like Briana, or funny like Sammy, doing all the computer work.

Sometimes I wonder what Jamila sees in me, she is so pretty. Her ebony skin and dark, sexy eyes make guys fall over themselves to get her attention.

But she chose me, and she helps me understand my feelings.

I am not alone.

Just breath in and out, remember the good times with everyone. It is strange to think that I didn't change much after the power station, unlike the others. I still had Jimy, and he protects me when the chips are down.

But where is he now? Strange. This is the situation he loves: a fight with someone just as big as him. Well, I can feel that this Mike fellow is hiding a little something.

Every time he touches me, I can feel something inside of him. Unbridled rage. Jimy has a lot of passion, but Mike has no restraint or meaning. Jimy uses his strength to protect and helps those who are helpless, me being one of them.

Jimy protected me when I couldn't, he was sturdy and durable. Didn't take any crap from anyone and we would run and run all day long together. It was fun, that was until we were kicked out of school because Jimy bashed a kid, but the kid was picking on me and throwing rocks as well, and Jimy jumped in and protected me. I love Jimy as much as Jamila. Well nearly as far, she is a breathtaking girl.

Come on Jimy, let's save everyone! Just think, he can't hear me. Where the bloody hell is he?

Even when we all were captured no Jimy came along to save the day but his last words to me. '**Jimy no like that place. Tell 'him' that it is a bad place, leave it alone.**'

He never refers to Ciro by his name, or anyone else.

The door screeches. Means only one thing. Mike is back.

They need to oil that.

Depowered

"So, da boss says I need to talk to you."

"Why should I talk?" *It seems odd he wants to talk to me,* "All you been doing is beating on me."

He follows that up with a punch in the gut.

Great talking. You wait until Jimy comes.

"Um, 'orry. Not supposed to do that." Mike pulls out a piece of paper. "They want to know, how are you healing?"

What kind of question is that? "Not sure… cause I do."

Screwing up his face, it turned purple. He raised a fist above his shoulder but doesn't follow through. "Listen, you answer and no hittin', ok?"

I try to shrug, and it does not work. "To tell you the truth, I always healed fast. I have always been strong, but not nearly as strong as my mate, Jimy."

He cocks his head at me. "Who dis Jimy?"

"He has been my friend for fifteen years, always got my back…"

Mike just laughs at me. "This Jimy bloke will come and help you? You are stupid." He just walks over, and for a split second, I swear I could see a bull's head.

I feel his fist slam into my side again. I hear a small crack. He caught one of my ribs. "Now, no

smart stuff. Question two, what were you lot comin'
'ere for?"

"Me and my friends?"

He takes his time squinting at the piece of
paper. "Yeah."

"Not sure. Ciro makes plans. My job is to make
sure Jimy comes along. Then he and I protect
everyone."

Mike snorts at that. "Did a good job, din't ya!"

"I tried, but I didn't see Jimy."

Laughing at that, he grabs my hair. Mike
smashes his fist into my face three times. Each time I
can feel my bones bend. The first, not a problem; the
second snaps my nose and blood gushes over my eyes
and drips off my eyebrows. The last one cracks my
cheekbone and breaks a tooth, and I feel like he
ripped some of my hair out as well. Mean bastard.

Mike starts to breathe like a bellows, in and out,
deep and loud like some kind of big animal. "That felt
good. Stupid face, now you have a flat face!"

Mike chuckles at his own words. I spit blood. I
hear something bouncing around the room. Must be
my tooth.

The swelling of my cheek makes me feel like I
have gone a full eighty-minute rugby game only
using my face to tackle. *Just you wait until I am free
Mike. I won't be using my face to hurt you!*

After a few moments, my thoughts come back
to me. "Mike, do you like hurting people?" I ask.

That look on his face makes me think that I just found uneaten chocolate at my house. What is the word I am looking for? So much joy. Ecstasy, yeah that's the word.

"Yeah, it's fun." Mike wipes my blood off his knuckles onto his overalls, "Breaking people is easy. Like baby kitty cats put in a sack, but you can take a few hits, you much more fun."

"Any more questions for me?"

He retaliates with a kick to my side, and I have to take a deep breath to block the pain like Sammy showed me. *James, you can survive this!*

"Shut up, Stupid!" he bellows. "Okay, I have more question. Three question. Why did you make FableLands? This is a stupid question, even Mike knows this one."

"I don't think Kayla made FableLands. It just is." Coughing a bit, that hurts. Ribs just cracked, not broken yet. "Kayla found the Lands, then Ciro made the device to connect to the Lands."

Not sure if I should be giving this away, but it is just general information. Nothing outstanding. I wish I Jamila were cuddling up to me right now, her warmth and company are just what I need.

Laying across the lounge at Jamila's place, watching some chick flick on tv. I wasn't caring about that, Jamila's long black hair just spread out over his lap. Only realising that this was my moment. This was true happiness.

I looked into Jamila's beautiful, serene face and mutters. "I love you…"

Jamila looks up away from the tv, her dark eyes filled with tears. Placing one ebony hand on my face. "I love you too, my gentle giant."

Of all the times thinking of that moment. Her love will see me through. No way I will break until I see my love again.

Mike is scratching his head with one hand, before pulling at my bonds as he looks at the sheet of paper in his other hand.

Not even a movement. What are these things made of?

I can break chains, but these ropes are super durable. I am not worried; Jamila or Briana will escape and find the rest of us. No way they could keep us.

Mike is really staring at that paper. Wonder if he is having issues reading. I have been there before, and it's painful. "Hey, Mike, can I help with reading the questions?"

"What?" His face again goes from being a motley of blues and reds to reddish-brown fur. What is this guy? "You stupid? Help me read?"

Mike throws down the scrap and strides forward. I know what is about to happen. Concentrate. Thump, left cheek. Whack, kidney. Thock, upper left chest. Another blow to the gut.

I grit my teeth to make sure no sound comes out. That gut punch did expel a bit of air, but he is so obvious as to where he will punch, and with Sammy's training I can prepare. This brute has no real skills, except strength and size. Jimy would wipe the floor with him.

Mike is leaning against the wall, breathing heavily. After a few moments, he calls out. "How'd you like that, stupid!"

"Fine," I say. Not so much, really, as he moved that rib bone with his chest punch, and it is harder to breathe. "Did you want help with that reading?"

He breathes through his nose, like a bull about to charge. "Teach you! I can read! You're the stupid one!"

He scrapes his right foot across the concrete floor, again and again.

"Come on, mate!" I plead. "I just want to help. The quicker we get through this, the quicker your boss-man is happy."

His foot stops mid-scrape. He stares at me like a deer in headlights. Grinning, he bends over and picks up the paper. "Ok," Mike walks over to me with the paper. "You read… and answer."

"Okay, the next question says-"

Because I am reading, I don't see the punch coming. My jaw rattles from the hit. Spots and my vision turn blurry. He follows up with another strike against the opposite side. I can't take this. Blackness takes me.

*   *   *

I was waiting around for the rest to arrive, looking at the factory from atop the cliff and arguing with the voice in his head. As I hear a familiar voice in my head, **Jimy thinks this is a bad plan! James will get hurt!**

"It's okay, Jimy. Ciro knows what he is doing."

Ciro too smart. Listen to me and gut. Gut says this bad.

Jimy does not notice the quicksilver form of his friend sidle up to him A quick tap on the shoulder, as he swings around with a fist high. It's just Sammy. "Hold your horses, big guy. Just your sexy mate, Sammy! What's happening?"

Gesturing down at the factory they are infiltrating tonight. I pointed out a few things to Sammy. "Guards are walking the perimeter, every second patrol has a dog, two towers with spotlights and most of the lights are on, and the chimney has been pumping out black smoke all night. If it weren't for the lights reflecting off it, I would never notice."

Sammy looks at my massive form, anyone looking at us would see two physical opposites. One is huge and muscular while the other is small and wiry. "Do you still have that feeling, James?"

"Not me Sammy. It is Jimy. Been yelling at me since we got here."

Sammy purses his lips. Looks up at the night sky, the stars of the universe just look back twinkling. "Maybe we should leave Jamila, Ciro and Kayla behind. You, me and Briana check this place out."

"We need everyone for my plan to work!" Ciro and the rest walk out from the darkness. I silently grimace. I didn't notice them either.

Briana comes along, laughing, rolling her shoulders and just getting into the moment. "Come on, we got this. Between Monkey, Jimy and George, they will protect the others and, if needed, slay any dragons."

I look up and sees my true love. All dressed in black, hair pulled back. She noticed me looking at her and flashes her pearly whites at me.

"Sweet beauty of love's first sight, only the two exist in the world. All around disappears and what is left is the song of forever." Kayla said smiling at them.

"Shut up, Kayla." Jamila says in a soft dreamy voice, eyes only for me, "He just a big oaf, but he is my big oaf!"

Jamila's voice makes me just want to ogle her more, lost in sight and sound of her.

"There he goes again, Sammy to James." I can hear laughter from the others behind me. "You need to calm down your sexiness, Jamila. James seems unable to function."

Our Jamila will get hurt in there. Jimy need to stop this!

Ciro knows what he is doing.

Jimy knows Ciro and Romulus are smart. Jimy leaves it in James' hands.

It took Ciro three clicks in front of my face to break his reverie. "Now, what is happening? Every detail will affect my plan. So, with as much detail as you can manage James: times, speed, numbers, and so on. Let's start with, what are the patrols like…"

*   *   *

"Oi! Wake up."

The words barely register before the water hits me in the face. The water washes into my nostrils, and I choke like I am drowning. Opening my eyes, there is Mike, empty bucket in hand and second one filled with water next to him.

"I am awake," I plead with him. "No more water."

Mike just grins as he bends over to pick up the bucket. I shake my head, but he throws it anyway. Being ready for it, I could turn my head and not be filled up with water.

His braying laugh echoes around the room, while I frantically turn my head back and forth blinking rapidly.

Mike turns the bucket over and squats down on it, using it as a stool. "Hah! Looks like you don't like water. Wants some more?"

"No. What is this, the latest version of your play time?"

He starts to scoff at that. "Nah. Hamill told me not to hit you anymore. Might kill you. So, he let me use water. I like seeing you struggle from the water. Almost as good as hitting you."

I watch him pick up a cloth and a hose. I am not looking forward to this. "So, what are…"

He whips the cloth over my head, and I cannot see anything. "Gonna plays a little game. You scream for me to stop and will stop. If you don't, I keep goin'."

His hand on the cloth pulls it tight on my face. Then suddenly, cold wetness engulfs my face. Wasn't so bad for a second, later the fabric became soaked, and water came through. Ever held your breath underwater and then a friend jokes around, then holds you under? Imagine that, but feeling like he will never let go.

Water fills up my nose, and I can't blow it out. Each time I try to breathe, it is like breathing into a wet sponge, just more water into my mouth. Even if I wanted to, I can't ask him to stop, and my restraints are not going anywhere.

The water stops and thankfully the cloth is removed. "You like the game?"

His grinning simpleton face is mere inches away from me. I cannot resist the opportunity. The crack of cartilage against my temple felt satisfying. "I like the game."

I just laugh at him when he clutched at his nose, trying to stem the flow of blood and smacking himself across the face with the end of the hose, stumbling back against the wall.

He throws down the hose with a stomp of his right foot, and his head and body begin to change.

Reddish-brown hair sprouts all over his body. His face extends into a broad snout, and two massive horns grow from his head. Do I see things? As Mike's body expands, his overalls rip, and the chest flap buttons pop off, and it now looks like a breechcloth.

"You gonna pay for dat!" Mike scrapes his foot across the floor, it is like watching a bull at the rodeo.

The Bull-man charges me with his horns pointing right at my throat. Bound as I am, there is no way for me to get out of the way. I cannot heal the amount of damage this will cause. I will die from this.

I don't know who smiled on me, but Mike trips on the hose he dropped. At the last second, the charge changes direction.

As the sharp horn pierces my bicep, the pain is intense enough to make me scream a little. Jimy has been stabbed before, but I haven't.

How could he stand this? I have to be brave like Jimy.

Mike backs off and whips his head up, and my blood sprayed from the wound and dripped down his now-red horn.

"Stupid hose." He curls up a massive fist and punches me in the chest. That rib and several others groan and crack under the strength of that blow, and it is enough to force to make me sway a tiny bit. "Looks like you need another."

With the vigour of a newborn kitten, I try and shake my head. If a bull could grin, this Mike-Bull did. As he raised his fist again, the door behind him opens.

"Stand down!"

Mike-Bull whips his head around, and a man in a lab coat walks in. Mike-Bull snorts at this new intruder. I am just glad I'm not getting punched again.

Jimy, where are you? I need you Jimy.

"But Dr Hamill!"

Just like Mike, this Hamill's head changes as well, into a tiger's. In an eerie voice, that makes my knuckles hurt, the Tiger replies, "You will do as I say, or I will carve you up into my supper, Minotaur!"

Jimy, help.

Split

Hamill-Tiger looks at him and pushes his right foot forward as if to dance. "Say you are sorry, bull."

Mike-Bull bows his head at the Hamill-Tiger then drops to his knees. "Yes, master."

Watching him crawl over and start licking the boot of this Tiger-man turns my stomach, or it could be from the pool of blood from the hole in my arm. Not sure.

Hamill's face turns back to normal, but it jumps again. From an old man with a grey beard, it turns into a woman with tight, blond hair, and then a young fellow that looks a bit like Briana but with a weird, neat haircut with shaved sides, combed over like a professional suit. Just odd.

It settles on the old man with a short, grey beard. "Where I am manners, I should introduce myself. My name is Dr Hamill. We have to stop that blood loss, first."

He walks over to a bucket with metal sticks in it. When he opens it up, a cheerful rosy glow comes from the bucket. I can feel the heat from here. He grabs one of the sticks, end glowing red, and Mike mutters something about being branded

Brace yourself. This will hurt, The words run through my head like a mantra as the glowing iron came closer.

The impact of hot metal created so much pain and a smell that I think I blacked out for a second. It's that voice that makes my knuckles itch that rouses me I guess.

"Nearly done!" he says, eerily cheerful. "Just the other side now." He drops the metal stick on the ground. Even though the end is no longer red, it hisses and sizzles in the pool of water and blood beneath me.

The puff of steam smells both coppery and irony. Like a steak oozing blood onto an iron skillet.

He grabs a second hot metal stick.

"Just a bandage will be fine," I heave. "I don't need another."

The old man-tiger smiles at that while licking his lips. Mike is still grovelling on the floor, and he starts to chuckle until Hamill clears his throat. He flinches down, fingers touching his shoulder where a large scar can be seen where hair does not grow. Some symbol that makes no sense. Ignoring my plea, he sticks the hot metal into the other side of my arm. The pain begins but goes numb to the touch. I can't feel much of my left arm now. What did he do?

"Now, a pleasure to meet you, James. My name is Dr Hamill. You can call me Dr Hamill or Doctor. I don't want you dead," *Yet, you mean I don't want you dead yet.* I thought to myself, "but I couldn't abide being disobeyed by one of my 'employees'. I am sorry for the pain, but it is helping us learn, which is for the greater good."

Mike now stands behind the doctor, all trace of horns gone, his head hung in shame. "Master, sorry. Not lose control again."

Hamill turns and pats Mike on the head. "I know you won't." Watching this exchange is weird. This whole thing is funny. Where is Jimy?

"Now, back to Mr Miller. So sorry… Blah-blah-blah. The question now is what to do with you, as I am impressed by your resilience."

"Where are my friends?" That sensation of itchy knuckles intensifies. "Tell me, and Jimy will be nice."

"Jimy? Jimy can't help you here. I can tell you, as you are the useless one of the group. We have built into the walls a type of harmonic that is the same amplitude as that place called the FableLands, but with an inverted phase. So: no calibration, no Arc. Simple." Ciro or Kayla would understand what this doc is talking about. "But do remember to call me Doctor Cornwall. Oh, Mike, a bit of punishment if you please."

Mike smiles his toothy grin again, cracking his knuckles as he moves towards me.

"Just the gut."

I can take it, just another gut punch. Just need to suck it in, and it should help. As I watch, he does an overhead hook, and I clench my stomach muscles to brace for the blow. Pain explodes, and my breath rushes out in a whoosh. That wasn't my gut, bastard punched me in the balls!

"Oh, Mike. Tsk. After this interrogation, I shall be looking at the video and see if you went too far. My apologies, Mr Miller. Mike is a bit of a brute." Still gasping for breath, a thought floats through my mind. *For every punch and hurt, Jimy will pay Mike back.*

"Where was I? Oh yes, why you are here. It is simple, to see how much you can endure."

After taking a few deep breaths, looking at this doctor through watery eyes, I ask. "Endure? You just want to see how much I can take..." The old man arches an eyebrow at me, with a sinister smile with it too, "Doctor?"

Mike is in the corner, looking for the red flag to start pounding away at my flesh. The doctor squats down, far more limber than his old face would be. He looks directly at me. "Yes. You are the muscle, so we're interested in what your limits in normal form are. Mike here is bound to an entity from FableLands. Not an Arc, but another mythical being, a monster. He still retains considerable strength and endurance even in his human form. Yet you are cut you off from your Arc. I want to know how much of the physicality comes from the connection, and how much is the host?"

"When can I start punching again?"

Mike looks like an impatient kid, bouncing back and forth on his toes. Tiger- Hamill turns and snarls at Mike. Just watching Mike flinch like that makes my heart warm. As Hamill turns back at me, his eyes are yellow and slit. He moves and starts to examine the red marks and bruising on my body. Being upside down, I have a great sight of his groin.

"Interesting, I have been watching the damage inflicted, but most injuries have already moved to proliferative phase or the maturation phase, remarkable." He moves to my arm. "See? This wound is already in the Inflammation stage. What would normally take hours or days, you are healing in a matter of minutes. Therefore, we need to hurt you. FableLands is such a tempting resource, far beyond our expectations. Mike, hold his head."

Mike comes over, placing his ham-hands on either side of my face. I can only see Hamill, on the edge of my vision. "Hold him still, Mike."

"Sure, Boss."

Sharp pain in my neck, I call out. "What…"

"Be still, son. One slip and you will never walk again." The pain stops. "You can let him go."

"What did you do to me?"

"Mike," the doctor calmly says. Mike slaps me hard across the face, which causes the pain from my neck to triple. "Remember, Mr Miller. Call me Dr Hamill."

Breathing in slowly. "I am sorry, Doctor Hamill, but what the fuck did you do to me?"

"Such Rudeness. The young today, so vulgar. I took a spinal sample from you. I will use them to have a few tests of your special powers."

"What sort of tests, Doctor?"

"Well, tissue and blood samples, healing observation and more stuff like that. Should take me a while…" Hamill slaps himself on his forehead. "I have to interview Subjects Four and Two."

Subject Two and Four. Who could those be? "Where are my friends, Doctor?"

"One moment James. I've never tried this, but my monster says I can do it."

As I watch, he turns into a Man-Tiger. At the same time, Mike, who has been slumped in a corner looking bored, stands up and changes into a giant Bull-Man.

Tiger-Hamill starts to vibrate. Faster and faster before my eyes, he becomes a blur, except for his teeth and eyes. One blur splits into three blurs. Each one slows down, and three Tiger-Hamills smile at each other.

The first one pipes up, with a feminine voice. "So, I have Subject Four." The Tiger turns into a stern woman with her blond hair in a tight bun. "He is the Trickster?"

Hamill Two, nods. With his toothy tiger mouth. Not understanding how he can talk with that cat mouth, I hear him say, "Yes, just watch it. Use the suit only if you must. Do not lose control."

"Sure."

I can tell that she is going to do what she likes. Lady Hamill turns and leaves. The third Hamill morphs into a pretty man? I think he is a man, not sure, and he looks familiar, but where from?

"I guess I have Subject Two. Fun, fun. The brutish thug, who thinks she is a knight," he breaks into a snobbish laugh. "Why not swap, I could keep 'experimenting' on this fine fellow."

The Older Hamill looks at the younger version. "The testing is nearly complete; your place is to manipulate Subject Two."

"Um, bosses, when can I go back ta hurting stupid 'ere?"

Mike speaks up, with a look of boredom on his face that he's held for the last ten minutes, not saying I am not in the same boat as him, but I hope they will let him just pound on me. It is easier to take than the cutting, and poking Hamill has done to me.

Both Hamills glare at Mike. There seems to be a not pleasant feeling in the air. These two give me the creeps. "You will have him when we are finished with the collecting," old Hamill turns to Young. "It is so hard to get smart workers these days."

Younger Hamill looks over at Mike, who's staring blankly into the corner. "We shouldn't have bonded him with such a creature. Didn't give him anything on the intelligence side."

"We need to unlock the larger monsters," he insists, as though trying to hammer home an old discussion "One of the dragons, or a decent-sized Chimera. They can be used in mass warfare. We are too subtle for that sort of destruction. Even Mike in full mode can't really hurt this depowered Arc."

They are losing me. I just want to have Jamila in my arms. *Jimy, where are you? I really need you now.* The old one points at me.

"What makes him so special? Such a remarkable level of Arc remains in the host, despite the harmonic concealer. There must be something in these samples. If not, the next step will be an autopsy."

"Call me up when you do that, guess I have to see to Subject Two. She's going to be fun, tootles."

Watching the younger version of Hamill makes me shake in fear of who Subject Two and Four are. To think about it, could that be Sammy and Briana? **I am going to rip their heads off!**

Jimy? That isn't him. Must be me thinking like him. This blocking stuffs! Getting pissed off!

Hamill looks over at me, "Just a couple more pricks and prods."

As he grabs another needle, an intercom lights up. "Doctor Hamill, your appointment with Rosemary is in ten minutes."

"Damn it! The succubus." As he stares at me, he talks, "Mike, take these samples to lab four. I will be back in a half-hour to finish." He sighs at me and turns to leave, still not looking at Mike. "Once you complete that, you can continue to 'subdue' him."

That got a look out of Mike. One of true happiness. "Right-o boss. Um, where is lab four again?"

I think I can hear Hamill whisper under his breath, 'utter moron,' but could be wrong. "Just follow the yellow line. Not the green, as that just takes you to the other interrogation rooms, the yellow line."

They have been spilling too much information in front of me. I might not be Ciro or Kayla, but it is easy to figure out I am not leaving this room alive.

Hamill leaves. "Very soon you are mine again, stupid," Mike laughs as I can see him gather all the samples and put them into a case.

He looks down at my face, "Almost got a real scream, not a proper one. Gonna make you scream for real when I get back."

He leaves. Watching him upside down is not a good look.

I need to get out of here!

Savage

*C*iro *is pointing towards me, motioning me forward towards the fence. I shouldn't be here; my frame is way too big to be hidden.* **Shut up, Jimy is here. Jimy will smash anyone who hurts the family.**

Thanks, Jimy for having my back.

That what Jimy is for!

Ciro in a whisper. "Now, Samuel you head to the top of the roof, and be our lookout while we cross the open."

Sammy looks at Ciro, "Are you sure?"

"Of course, I am sure. There will be a break in the patrols for thirty-seven seconds. The lights will be facing the other way for forty-three seconds. That is our window."

Kayla, along with Jamila and Briana, are all in black.

Damn, Jamila is so sexy right now. That skin-tight costume. Jamila sees me staring at her, she shakes her head and smiles. Whoops! Need to think about the plan.

"Um, Ciro?" I pipe in.

Like usual, Ciro rolls his eyes as he answers. "Yes, James."

"You sure that I won't be spotted? I'm pretty big."

Ciro sighs and grabs his face. "We have gone over this for…"

"Brother, calm down," Kayla comes over and places her hand on me. Briana is warming up her body, and Sammy is climbing up the wall. "It will be fine, the energy is flowing well, my giant friend. Just remember to embrace your Jimy if it seems to be going the wrong way."

Already here, little sister.

Kayla has a slight giggle. I smile down at her. "Sorry, just have a bad feeling."

Jamila comes over too, kisses me on my cheek. "James, don't worry. My pheros are out, and I can deal with any guards that we overlooked."

"We are lucky to have you." I lean in and whisper in Jamila's ear, "So am I."

Giving her a quick peck, too, I head over to the wall and stand there waiting to boost everyone over.

*   *   *

I am going to get out of these restraints! Just like doing those upside-down crunches, like I seen on the telly. If I can just get the leverage on these cords, I can get out.

One, two, hmm.

Again, just need to bring my arms up again.
One, two, now!

 Maybe bring my legs in too. Give that a go…
One, two…

That was like five hundred crunches. Must keep it up. Bloody cords don't even feel like they are moving. Just keep it up, this might bring Jimy along. Okay, number five hundred and one, two…

Crack!

What was that? After this Jamila will love my new ab workout!

Now. One two, come on! That was another crack!

Hang on that sounds like the concrete cracking. Where is Ciro when I need him? He would know all that smart stuff on how much strength I need for breaking concrete.

Just need a break, my abs are killing me.

Hearing a noise, I look up to see Mike walk back in.

Saying walk is an understatement. He is bouncing with joy.

"I'm back, dumb-dumb. Time to dish out some pain!" He bounds over and slugs me in the gut. I let out a grunt and a whoosh. Why in the gut? "Oh, you felt that one. One for Mike!"

"Just caught me off-guard, Mike."

"I did, really?" Mike starts to walk around me, having an eye full of his groin each time he moves around me. "So catching off-guard works, hey?"

"No-"

He punches me in the gut again, letting out a squeak and a grunt. My whole ab region is like it is on fire. I haven't rested enough to deal with this.

"What, you a little mousey? Squeak, Squeak!" Mike walks around me again, laughing. Need to steady my breath. I have a way out, just need him to leave again. "So that is how you hurt? This is turning into the best day ever!"

A sharp pain from my back radiates from my kidneys, and I nearly let out a yelp of pain. Damn him!

"Surprise! So close, nearly a real scream. Time to put on my real face!"

In front of me, he morphs into a bull-man, but this time is different. He grew not just in height, but also in width. His eyes turn red, and there seems to be a red mist coming out of his now-bull nostrils, his hands are the size of hams, and his whole body is covered in a reddish-brown fur. Looking down, his boots have burst out, and what is left is hooves.

I've seen him with the bullhead, but this reminds me of when Jimy is around. Vast and savage. Jimy is a noble savage while 'Mike' is just feral looking.

"Mike, are you still there?"

I am becoming worried about him. Just now, I can hear Ciro's voice just lecture 'Are you stupid, James? This creature is not worth your time.' You can say that, but I can't change who I am. This is wrong, and Mike isn't here anymore. There is no humanity in those soulless eyes.

"Shuddup, 'Tard!"

The once-Mike bellows at me, and as he charges he brings his horns down. He is going to impale me. At the last moment, he lifts his head and wallops me in the gut, following it up with a furred knee to the face. My right eye closes up. Again, he brings in his ham-sized fist into my rib cage, this time with a snap, and I'm finding it hard to breathe.

Closing my eyes, I start calling to Jimy, trying to ignore the pounding of my body. I don't think I can take much more. I have to find him.

"Jimy! Jimy! Where are you?"

I find myself in an empty corridor, each side filled with doors. Maybe one of these will lead me to Jimy?

All I can do is try.

Door number one? Nope, locked. Door two sealed as well. Reaching the third entry, which looks like my old bedroom door; it is closed and bolted too.

Screw this, grabbing the door handle, leaning in and throwing my weight against the door. Hearing a crack, I do it again. The door splinters and it opens into a void, a place of pure darkness.

Yelling into the void. "JIMY! ARE YOU THERE?" Nothing. I have a feeling this is the place, but it must be that interference Tiger man talked about. "Jimy! I am here! Where are you!"

Again, no answer.

I can feel my body dying. If I can't find Jimy now, it is over. I need to be brave like Jimy and step into the void. Stepping off the edge, I hear something from the back where my body is.

Someone has entered the room. I hope it is Hamill.

As I opened one eye, I see it is Jamila and someone else. The woman with Jamila looks weird, with long black hair and two red horns on her forehead. Her feet are hooves, like Mike's, and she has two bat-like wings sprouting from her back. Two black eyes with red slits and razor teeth finish off the package. The smell of sulphur and brimstone is in the air.

Seeing Jamila, all I can do is smile, even though my cracked lips ooze more blood, but who is that guy with a gun on her?

Don't you hurt my Jamila!

Keep smiling.

Jimy I need you now! Jamila is in trouble!

Bull-Mike turns and grunts at the weird lady. "What you doin' 'ere!"

"Come now, Mikey, just here to create a new monster. Leave his sack of meat to us, we will make him squeal!"

A low chuckle comes from the Bull-Man. "If you do, record it. Been workin' on 'im for ages now. Not a decent peep! Bloody 'Ero!" He spits on me and laughs as he leaves. "This be good to watch! But I hungry!"

Good, I don't think my body could handle any more.

"Stupid cow. But Mike does have his uses," She points at me and speaks, though not to the guard, to Jamila. "Now, for your final test."

I can't quite understand what is happening here, but Jamila looks so pretty. But I can see that this isn't right. Maybe me calling out to Jimy will, "Ji.."

Nope, only a spasm of coughing happens, and blood gushes out of my mouth, falling into my eye and blurring my vision. *JIMY!!!*

There must be a way to get to him… **What?**

"Now my apprentice, the last test is simple. To see if you really let go and want to step onto the other side, you need to watch me kill him. Your love, so sweet but a waste of time."

Jimy is that you?

Yeah, what you want Jimy for?

"Tut, tut. If you fail, then you both die, slowly. You first."

Look, Jamila is in trouble!

Jimy can't see. It is all red and black.

Okay, have blood in my eye. I will try, Jimy.

Opening my eye, it is tinged with red, but I can make out… there is a gun pointed at Jamila's head! Feeling Jimy in my head, we let out a savage snarl!

No, hurt our Jamila! Tell Jimy why Jimy can't move. Why Jamila upside-down?

Ropes are holding us the wrong way up.

Bah, Jimy will be free!

"Enough, foolish man. Those restraints can hold 6 tons each, comfortably." **Stupid lady, Jimy no care! Let Jimy out!** "I will show you how to do this later."

"Stop this, I can control him. There is no reason to kill him!"

"I guess punishment is in order," she shrugs, then addresses the guard. "Shoot her knee out."

What! *What!* ***We kill a bad person, we need to free ourselves.*** *Jimy you have control.* **JIMY BE FREE!**

I can feel Jimy taking over. I am feeling stronger. *Jimy pull!*

Jimy nos that!

I will help, too.

I can hear the ground and roof crack and break, like listening to the tearing open of the stone.

"Point the weapon at the Demon!"

Jamila smart. Jimy will be free soon.

"No, point your gun at her!"

No, Jamila, we both call out.

We pull on the ropes again. There seems to be some slack in the cable. Nearly there.

"No! You have no power here, Demon!" I hear Jamila call out.

"You think your Arc can save you? You are like me. Give in, Jamila."

Yes, we can save her!

"If you don't, I will kill your James."

We start to yank on the ropes, again and again. This time there is a huge crack and the anchors in the ceiling break, and we fall to the ground. "Kill that witch!"

We stand up and bend over and rip each rope from the ground with just a flexing of our shoulders. "Give in, Demon," Jamila demands.

The look in the stupid guard's eye seeing our true form makes him lose his shit.

"You are free."

The guard drops his gun, stares behind the Demon at us and runs screaming into the wall. "Your man is still trapped!"

The weird woman spins around and looks at us, the colour drops from her face.

Marilyn's voice can be heard. "Have you meet my boyfriend, Jimy?"

Standing over her, we bellow and raise out a mighty fist, **"You leave Jimy girl alone!"**

We swing our fist at the weird-looking woman. Jimy must be really angry. The weird woman's head flies off and smacks into the wall with a wet crunch.

Jamila's face is full of tears. She runs over and grabs our waist. "James, you are…"

She breaks into tears. **"Jimy here."** We embrace her, smelling her scent. She has been in trouble. **"Where others?"**

Looking up at us, "I don't know, James. I love you and Jimy."

Holding up our arms, **"How Jimy get out of this?"**

Our love looks at the connection of these ropes. "It seems to be knotted onto your wrists and ankles. Just one moment…"

We look at the right joint, grab the line, and pull. We rip it over our oversized hand, taking a lot of skin with it. Grunting, we watch as the flesh heals straight away.

"James, just wait! Look what you have done." Our beloved gathers a pink cloud in her hands and presses it against our wound. "Now, no more doing silly things, there must be something around here to help with the knots. Something small, but strong."

We flex our right hand. It's alright now. **Jimy wants out still.**

Just give Jamila a little time, Jimy. She is smart, she'll find something to help with the knots.

Hope James is right.

Looking at her backside wiggling around is making us feels flustered, but no time for that. "This will do." Holding it up, a thin bit of metal. "Come here, James."

She hugs us again.

Jimy, tell her to follow the green lines.

"Um, James says to follow green lines." Why Jimy say that?

We follow lines, takes us to the others, Jimy.

Jamila says. "What are the green lines?"

"Um, James says if Jimy and Jamila follow, lead to others." *Good, Jimy.*

"Well, with you, James, we will find the others. Let's go."

Green

We all leave the room like always, squeezing through and bending over. Getting through the door frame is hard. Why is Jimy so big? **Cause Jimy is!** He still says to me.

Walking into the corridor makes me shiver in the starkness of the sterile white walls, but I can make something out. A dead guy in the hallway, his brains splatted against the wall.

Jimy laughs a little at that, he does have a refreshing sense of humour.

"So, we follow the green line that will take to the others, but which way?"

Hmm, what you think Jimy? **Jimy no care, Jimy wants out!** *Move over Jimy, let me talk to Jamila.* **Ok.**

"My love, if Jimy and I head left, and you head right-" **No, Jimy stays with Jamila.** *Jimy she can protect herself, and we need to split up to find others.* **No, Jimy Jamila.** "Sorry, Jimy wants to stay with you," I say, shaking my head. "So, do I, but we need to be quick."

"I know, James," she reaches up on her tippy toes to brush her hand across my face. "But I need to find Sammy. He is in trouble. We need to find the medical bay first. So, if green is holding rooms, what do yellow and red mean?"

Yellow means lab. "That one leads to labs. Could be the same thing with the medical section. Not sure what the red or the blue one is."

"Okay," she nods with her natural vitality. "As long as the yellow and green follow each other, we will stay together, but once they separate we have to as well. Okay, James?"

I can feel Jimy frown, but I say to him. *Listen to Jamila, she is smarter than us.*

"Okay, Jamila. Jimy listen. You smart!"

"It is going to be okay, James. You first. We need to move."

Jimy and I start walking fast, with Jamila jogging down the hallway behind us, each of our shoulders touching either side. At least this will give Jamila cover if someone has a gun. I can see that up ahead there is a T-section. The green and yellow head right while the red and blue line head left.

We move up and look around the corner. There are two guys with guns coming from the left. Jimy breaks into a run. **"Jimy smash!"**

After a little shock, they raise their guns and fire. The sensation of needles hitting the skin. Swing our massive fist into one of the guards, and his mouth spews blood as his body buckles under our strength. We then sweep around for a backhand blow, but Jamila calls out.

"Wait, James! We need information." We look over and snatch the firing gun out of the guard's hand. "Pin him against the wall, James."

Smiling at this, knowing what our Jamila will do, Jimy obliges, **"Sure, Jimy do."**

We grab the guy by the throat then quickly lift him off the ground and pin him against the wall.

Jamila walks over. She gives us shivers when she walks like that. So beautiful our Jamila is, the ebony skin glowing in the fluro lights.

"Now my lovely, look at me," she says to the soldier, before turning to me. James, could you remove the mask?" Ripping off the mask, the face underneath looks like from that old show, Walking Dead. So ugly. "Aren't you interesting?" she quirks an eyebrow. "Just a simple question. Where is the medical area?"

I can smell roses in her hair. I love the smell of her hair. He looks not that nice at Jamila. **Jimy no like that look.** We start to squeeze; the guard begins to squirm in our grip.

"Jimy! Let him go, now!"

Oh no, Jamila is angry at us. Dropping the guy, we look down at our feet. **"Jimy sorry, Jamila."**

"It is okay, Jimy and James. I have him under my control, now. Give him space and watch the corridor, okay?"

Nodding our head, **"Sure, Jimy do."**

We should get angry. Jamila is powerful but not like when she stared at us when we did something stupid, that is scary. "Now, where is the medical area?"

His pupils have expanded to the point that there is no colour bit of the eye. I have seen this before on people under her control. "The blue is for medical, red is for the armoury, yellow for labs and green for cells."

"See, wasn't that easy? Now, sleep."

The guard slumps to the floor. Looking at our beloved, **"Now what Jimy do?"**

"Well, James and Jimy, you head towards the cells, and I head towards the medical area. Hopefully, I can save Sammy."

"Jimy like that. Sammy friend."

She pats our arm and shivers run up it. My green tattoos glow in response. "This is where we part ways for a while. Once I find Sammy, we will catch up."

It will be alright, she seems a little different now. Our love will be okay by herself. **"Jimy no wants this, but James says you will be good. Jimy loves Jamila."**

"I love the both of you too."

We watch her jog away down the hallway. *Now, Jimy. Let's find the others.* **Jimy wants that, too. And smash some people. Maybe find Bull-man, also!** *Maybe, Jimy. I want to have words with him as well.* **Is that fist words? Jimy is good with fist words.**

Looking down, we start to follow the green path.

War

As we move down the hall I wanted to know what happened to Jimy for all those times I called out to him. Following this green line, hoping we will bump into the others.

So Jimy where you been?

What you mean? Jimy always here.

No, Jimy before we were captured you disappeared. You have always been there but not when Jamila was in real trouble.

Jimy no understands, Jimy always here for Jamila and James. Jimy can't member.

I know it pointless to keep asking Jimy where he was, he is here now, and that is all that matters.

In the distance, we can hear gunfire, like echoing popping sounds. We need to move, that could be one of our friends in trouble.

As we change our walk into a sprint, our shoulders keep hitting the sides of the walls and creating significant divots in the concrete. *We need to be careful, Jimy!*

Why? Stupid walls are too close.

Sometimes it is hard when Jimy has control, he doesn't quite understand that things break really easy around him. The gunfire is becoming even more intense and now mixed with the rapid sounds of a woman yelling. Could that be?

Move Jimy, Briana or Kayla might be in trouble!

We speed up, not caring this time about the damage we are causing, the floor cracks under the power of Jimy's bounding steps. In the distance, five soldiers are firing down the hall.

Yelling out **"Jimy Smash!"** we charge down.

One of the guards realise that we are moving at pace towards him, turns and we hear a FRRRRRRRRAK, as he turns and shoots. The air shattered in the wake of his barrage. The bullet tore through space, and we feel it hit our skin, like heavy rainfall. Like watching in slow motion, the desperate, frantic firing as we backhand him into the others. As we move over the fallen soldiers, we stomp down on their prone bodies, snapping limbs and ribs.

The hallway is clear. "Thanks for the help, Jimy." We know that voice, it is Briana!

There she stands, clad in her light armour holding her bright sword casually in her hand. **"Lookie its Ana!"**

"Good to see you too, big guy. Can I talk to James for a moment?"

"Um, sure."

Flying into the forefront of our collective consciousness, "Hi Briana, Jimy and me are happy you are safe."

Leaning on her sword, the floor melts slightly around the tip of it. "Have you found any of the others?"

"Yes, Jamila found me, and she knows where Sammy is, but we found out that these green lines will bring us to the other cells."

As we all look down at the green line, Briana points down the corridor that we haven't been down. "No point going where I've been, we should go that way."

Jimy pushes me out of the way, he like Briana, a fellow protector. **"Jimy says yes!"**

Briana pulls her sword out of the ground and starts to jog down the hallway. "Let's go."

"Yeah." *Yeah!*

Moving down, Briana's body still clad in her armour, sometimes we wish we had armour because it looks cool. "Jimy, what happen to you? Are you okay?"

"Jimy fine. Why Ana want to know? Jimy can't remember what happened."

Briana pats our arm, "It is okay, things happened to me that I would like to forget."

As we turn another corner, three guards are standing in front of a massive door. I can feel Jimy wanting to charge down and smash these goons. "One moment, Jimy, we need to give them a chance to surrender," Briana calls down to the three. "Lay down your weapons, and you will not be hurt."

One of the mask men yells back, his voice has a weird metallic tone to it. "That is our line, but please resist, it is boring guarding this door!"

They move towards us, guns snapping to aim at us. Briana turns to me and bows. "After you Jimy."

Jimy grins at that, looks at the three men. **"Jimy going to have some fun too!"**

As we charge in swatting away at the barrage of bullets heading our way, I can tell that Jimy finds this all too easy. With a sweep of his arm, he smashes one guard into the wall, with enough force to send out shockwaves and damage the concrete. I could smell the acidic aroma of wee on the second guard as it trickles down his leg as Jimy steps and brings down his massive fist. Snapping out with his left hand, Jimy grabs the last guard, and with barely a flick tosses him into the door.

"Jimy, you could have left me some!"

"Jimy sorry Ana. Ana think friends in there?"

As I watch Briana look at the door and the keypad next to it, I say to Jimy. *Jimy, how are you going?*

Jimy fine. Angry, want to hurt these bad men.

I know, Jimy but don't lose yourself. If you need me to take back over just ask.

James is too soft now, Jimy will make wicked men pay.

There is no talking to him, Briana looks up from the keypad. "I don't know how to unlock this, could you open it for me?"

"Jimy do!"

Strolling up to the door, we swing a punch at the door, following up with a kick. That seems to be loosening it, so we try again. Each shock vibrates the wall, and the door starts to shake loose. We grab the corner of it and tear it from its hinges.

We walk in and see Kayla strapped to a chair, and she is sleeping, but the smell in the room is like cooking meat. Briana pushes pass us. "Oh my Lord, Kayla!" She runs over, her sword shrinks to a length of a small knife. "Jimy, we need to find Jamila!"

"What wrong?"

Briana cradles Kayla, brushing her hair off her face, her eyes full of tears. "She has been badly burnt, they have been hurting her!"

What? We are going to kill them all, Jimy! **"Jimy and James will find and kill all bad men!"**

I couldn't contain myself, taking control of our arm, I smashed our fist into the wall. Cracks form and a crater expand from our strike. Briana stands next to us. "This is not the time, Jimy. We need to find Jamila."

"She is in the medical area, Jamila went there to find Sammy. We have to follow the blue lines."

"James?" Briana looks at me with surprise. "Okay, let us go find her. Should you let Jimy be in control again, in case we bump into bad guys?"

Jimy want to smash everyone! "No, he is too angry to think beyond smashing everyone. I will be fine being your back up. Give me Kayla, I can hold her in one arm."

As Briana hands over Kayla, I cradle her in my forearm. It feels different being in control and in my Arc form. His strength is immense and scary, even though it is my body, just strange. I can hear him screaming and smashing creative things in my mind. Once he calms down, I can let him back out.

Briana squeezes my arm, "Move, there is the blue line."

We pick up the pace, Briana is jogging at my side, and I am just taking giant steps. The speed of this body too, what would I be like in an open field? I would run faster than a bear but not a cheetah, I don't think. Would be interesting.

As we reach another T-section, the blue line splits and goes both ways. Briana looks up at me and asks. "James, which way now?"

As I take a deep breath through my nose down each hallway, I can smell Jamila's lovely aroma, it like freshly cut flowers in spring. To the left is the strongest.

"That way." I start to head down with Briana following and Kayla. Looking down at Kayla, her breathing has stopped. "Briana, there is something wrong with Kayla."

Briana comes over and touches her face and then wrist. "We need to find Jamila now! If we run into someone, charge through!"

Not even replying, I start a run, moving towards the most potent scent of my beloved. Nothing will get in my way! **Jimy agrees!**

I could see just ahead of another group of soldiers, pointing their guns at me. Turning my shoulder to them so the gunfire will just bounce off my back and not hit Kayla, then I charge through the pack.

Stomp them! Jimy wants to stomp! *No, Jimy, Briana will finish these evil men, we need to get to Jamila for Kayla's sake.*

Sending them flying as I hit the pack at full speed. Behind me I could hear the sizzle of Briana's sword, warping the air around it due to the intense energy pouring off it.

Not glancing back, I take another deep breath, and the scent of my beloved is close. Look down the hall I notice that the blue line turns into an open-door frame. She must be in there!

Ducking under the doorframe into a sterile room, with steel benches with bodies draped with white cloth. In the middle is my Jamila standing with bright flashes surrounding her body, the most beautiful sight I have ever seen. On the metal slab is a naked Sammy. His body is black and oozing, with every pass of Jamila's hand, the skin had a fresh tan look and joined with each passing of the side was a flash of light like a camera flash.

I stood in awe of my love, she will always be my beloved forever. "Why are you just standing there!" Briana calls out behind me. "Oh, we'll wait. I will keep watch." The sound of her footsteps echoing out of the

With one last pass of Jamila's hand, all of Sammy's skin was healed. She turns and sees Kayla in my arm. It was the most beautiful sight I have ever seen, her hair and shirt catching on an imaginary breeze. Flashes of light, like cameras trying for that perfect picture. Only this sight is indeed for me.

"Bring her over here." Jamila points to a free table. "What happened?"

Briana steps back in as she notices that I am at a loss for words, "It seems that she somehow melted the nylon straps into her skin, but there was no flame only two smashed light bulbs." After Briana says that, she steps back outside.

I moved out of the way, looking over at a naked but confused Sammy. I look around and see a pile of clothes, pick up a bunch and trudge over to his table. "Here put some clothes on, the girls are present." **Yeah, Jamila is Jimy's!**

He blinks and smiles. "You sure that isn't what they really want to see?"

A quick call from outside, "I don't think so, Sam."

As he pulls on a pair of trousers that are a little big for him. "You are sure, Briana?" He laughs again, Sammy always calms my nerves. "So, what has been happening?"

"You don't remember?" **What's wrong with Sammy?** Jimy has that right, something is off with him. "We were captured, and you were really burned."

"Hmm, can't remember. Oh well,"

Sammy extends his hand, and a staff jumps out. Then pulls a bunch of hair out of his head. Then blows it away, fifteen copies of Sammy are standing there. I have never seen him do this before.

"Okay, you lot, go find an exit. Travel in packs of three. Go!"

All I hear is 'Yes, boss!' as they run out of the room pass Briana. "How did you do that?"

Sammy blinks at me, "It felt right, not sure how but it was right."

A high soft voice from behind Sammy and I. "Where is Ciro?"

Swivelling around, we see Kayla sitting up, with Jamila leaning heavily on the table, and my beloved's legs seem to be giving way. Ignoring the question, I rush over and wrapping Jamila into my arms, kissing her gently on the head. "You can rest now Jamila."

A sleepy smile escapes her lips as she falls asleep in my arms. Sammy is just hugging Kayla. "James, Briana, where is Ciro? I can sense he is in trouble!"

That brings me out of my fixation of Jamila's ebony face. Briana comes in too, the sword of light still drawn. She asks. "Do you know where Ciro is, Kayla?"

As I watch her close her eyes and start waving her hands in the air. Every so often it looks like she hits a solid wall. **Worse than white face man Jimy saw once.**

Shh, Jimy, rest we will need you soon.

I can still hear my friend grumble at the edge of my thoughts. Kayla slowly opens her eyes. "He is thirty meters at North twenty-two degrees west. His energy flow has become erratic, he could be in danger."

I am completely dumbfounded by these directions if they are that at all. **What Kay talking about, Jimy no understands.**

The other three stares at each other, shrugging. Sammy speaks up. "Hey, Kayla where is north? Sort of remember this from PE but not that much."

Kayla just smiles at Sammy, "Don't worry Sammy, it is this way."

As we move out of the medical bay, Sammy takes the back, Jamila leaning on Kayla, and the both of them are in the middle. Briana in front and I am following right behind. Kayla calls out. "Take the next left."

Jamila taps me on the shoulder. "There are five-gun men around the right corner."

Jimy pushes me aside and puts Jamila gently on the ground. **"Jimy got dis!"**

We charge towards the group of faceless men, all their guns trained at us. I could feel a presence next to us. Briana, with her sword all alight, running beside me. We smash each guard within our reach, with Briana protecting our flanks. Barely a shot fired from these soldiers, something is nagging at my thoughts, but as soon as the violence stops, that fleeting thought floats away.

"Jimy like to smash!"

Briana looks down at the fallen, picks up one of the guns. Ejects one of the clips, and sees that there are no bullets. "Yes Jimy, but this seems to be becoming easier and easier with each encounter. Let's get back to the others."

Jimy nods our head, but I retreat a little, thinking about that empty gun. This feels wrong, but I can't put my finger on why.

Briana catches up with Kayla with the empty clip in her hand. "What do you take from this?"

Handing the clip to Kayla, "Someone or something is working for us, but it is unclear what their true motives are yet. Once we find my brother, we shall flee and talk about what has happened to us when we are safe."

Kayla points again down another corridor, we move down there as one. My beloved is leaning on Kayla, and they seem to be in deep conversation. **Don't listen, Jimy thinks it is rude!**

I wasn't going to listen, just worried about her. She has done more this afternoon that she has ever done before.

She is strong! That is why Jimy and James love her!

So true.

Kayla calls out. "Ciro is in that room," Just like all the other rooms, a heavy steel door. There is a catch in Kayla's voice I didn't notice before. "Jimy, James, we need to get in, my brother is in danger!"

Don't need to tell us twice. *Ready Jimy, the both of us!*

I could feel Jimy reeling from this thought. He just sends me a mental grunt. As we clinch our hands together and raise them overhead. We shatter the concrete ceiling as our double fist cleave a colossal gouge into it. Bring our whole weight behind this, the air itself cracks like thunder from the swing.

As we have never used this much strength before, the door in slow motion buckles and breaks away from the wall then flies into the room. Kayla pushes past me, and as we squeeze into the room behind her, we see a blueish black liquid spreading out from the door. To one side is Ciro, his olive complexion, white with fear. In his hand is a chair and a pen with the same liquid dripping off it.

Kayla says to him. "Ciro, are you alright? We are here to save you!"

"Jimy help too."

Ciro just drops the chair and pen, without saying anything to us walks out of the hole. "Briana, we need to leave."

In Briana's arms is Jamila, I am starting to feel sorry that I am not looking after her. "It is happening as we speak, Sammy has sent out scouts to find an exit." She seems to be looking at something. We lean in and have a look too. "Are you okay?"

"I am fine," Shaking his hand at us. "I was in the process of escaping, and you ruined it."

Kayla steps up and scowls at Ciro. "You were not! If Jimy didn't do that, that monster would have grabbed you." Kayla's face is losing all colour. "What happens to your nose?"

"Enough sister, we can discuss this when we escape."

Briana allows Kayla and Ciro to take up the responsibility caring for Jamila. We take a step forward, wanting to be the one doing it. Briana looks up at us. "No, Jimy we need you in front. No-one is as strong or resilient as you." We nod our heads, pushing through to the front again. Briana calls out. "Sammy, which way to the exit?"

Sammy giggles in the background. "Really simple, just straight down there. The rest of my brood will keep the soldiers occupied so we can flee." He pulls another clump of hair out, blowing on it another ten Sammys appear. "Go have some fun!"

All of them laughing, they run off in groups of two in different directions. Briana points down the hall. "Let's go."

We all pick up the pace, running down the hall. It seems that the extra Sammys have taken out some more guards, as we pass several knocked down, bleeding from head wounds.

Just ahead of us is a door, sturdy but nothing compared to what we have been dealing with for the interrogation rooms. Breaking into a run with our shoulder moving into a ramming position, we charge the door. As we smash through, the crispiness of the night washes over us. The stars are bright and twinkling at us. As we scan the darkness, there is a sort of sameness surrounding the compound.

Briana and Sammy step up next to us, Sammy takes in a breath. Briana extinguishes her blade and says. "We are in a desert."

Epilogue of Interrogation

Hamill is staring at his security feed of the mayhem that is created by the Arcs. Across from him are his two counterparts, John and Jane.

"Look at this!" Hamill says to the other two. "We couldn't have planned it better. We shall send this video to the police, and our sweet 'heroes' will be hunted. I love character assassination almost as much as real assassination."

John looks up at the wall where the real Dr Hamill's corpse is nailed to the wall. He smiles and licks his lips. "Stupid human, thinking that he can control us. And now we have corrupted this generation of Arcs. Escaping FableLands is only the beginning, but we need to perfect the transfer."

Jane looks at the schematics of Ciro's Device. "Wishing we got more, but, unlike us, the others are too unstable to be of any use other than fodder."

Hamill hops up and moves over to the corpse, carving off a chunk of flesh and brandishing it in his hand. "True, but we have time now." He heads back to his chair. "Look at this. The power of the Giant. Three blows on that reinforced door, and it flies off the hinges."

Jane looks up at the plans and studies the monitor. "Yes. The Lover is quite powerful too, but I think Rosemary broke her. Watch as she revels in the use of her powers. Soon, she will become like us."

John is looking at his tablet, "I wish I had more time with the Knight. If we broke her, it would break the team."

After taking a bite of his snack, Hamill grunts at John. "Hmm… you, John, created an illusion to finish interrogating her. If you had been there, we might have been successful."

John looks up from the tablet at Hamill, sucking air through his teeth. "Why did you send in that Aswang in with the Founder?"

Jane looks away from the screen, too, her eyes glowing from the refection of the security feed. "I would like to know, too."

"It was a gamble and didn't pay off. Being manipulated by a human, even if they are an Arc, is why she is dead."

John taps on his tablet, "Look at this." What pops up on the screen is the Knight, glowing in armour made of light and holding her sword of pure energy. "Why didn't our countermeasures work? She is in full mode. Scary."

As the Knight's sword cuts through guards like a scythe through grain harvest. Then in mere moments, she meets up with the Giant, and they both go on a rampage of grisly proportions.

Jane pipes in, "How did the Lover resurrect the Trickster?"

Hamill and John snarl at that, both their gazes exposing their true selves: Rakshasa.

Hamill's voice is like a thunderous storm. "If you could have controlled yourself for a moment, that wouldn't have happened. Why did you lose control?"

Jane smiles cattily at the two men. "Because I wanted to."

John shakes his head and then laughs. "You wanted to! I wanted to as well, but the plan…"

Hamill nods his head at this. Jane rolls her eyes, which looks out of place with her clean appearance. "The plan? The plan is working. It is right there on the screens."

Hamill still does not look amused. "Granted that your loss of control didn't affect our overall plan, but you were close being returned to the FableLands."

Jane stands up abruptly, her chair flinging to the other side of the room. Her face morphs back into her demon form, a humanoid tiger. "You think you could send me back? Come on old man!"

Hamill leans back in his chair. "You want a fight? I have not lived for these countless years to give up my chance to be corporeal again." Looking behind her, the back wall shimmers, and a minotaur is standing there. "That is why we have minions, my dear."

With two quick steps, the colossal creature snatches up Rakshasa-Jane before she could react, and with a twist of his wrist, the Minotaur breaks her neck. Dropping the body down, it now assumes its original shape of a middle-aged woman with greying hair.

"Did I do good?"

Hamill nods. "Yes, Mike. You did exactly what I wanted, but I am still disappointed in you about your lack of control when it came to the Giant."

Bull-Mike lowers his snout in shame, "I'm sorry, Mr Hamill. He pissed me off! He still lives."

"Yes, he does. But it was a close one. If I hadn't dropped the interference in that room, he would have died from your inflicted injuries."

John taps his foot impatiently. "So, back to the plan." He looks over his shoulder at Mike. "You can leave us, Mike."

"Yes, Mr John."

John leans forward. "Except for a few hiccups, the plan went well. The Arcs are escaping, and we have footage of their violence and murder, as well as their trespassing on company grounds."

Hamill laughs at this. "Yes. A little bit of torture and they forget who they are."

"So, shall we begin stage three? Our next candidates are ready for bonding."

Hamill looks back on the monitors, watching the six break out of the facility. From the Giant's strength to the Lovers control and the Knight's leadership, their escape would have happened even if it wasn't set up. What was remarkable was the duality of the Trickster, the reality manipulation of the Genius, and the pure mind of the Founder. These six would be formidable if they weren't ten steps behind the company.

With everything in place, Hamill just smiles at the real outcome of this adventure.

"Of course. Let us begin."

The End of FableLands: Interrogation.
Keep an eye out for FableLands: Fugitive, in 2018.

For updates on the series FableLands; Journal of an
Adventurer, Tales From Favinonia or Àodàlìyǎ, the
land that never was,
you can follow the author on

Facebook
(https://www.facebook.com/scolbranauthor)
Twitter
(https://twitter.com/SamuelAuthor)
Instagram
(https://www.instagram.com/samuelauthor)

Please remember to leave a review on Amazon!

Cover for FableLands is commissioned from
Julia Raymond.
To see more of her work head over to:
https://www.shootingstarshooter.com

www.ingramcontent.com/pod-product-compliance
Lightning Source LLC
Chambersburg PA
CBHW060746210726
48292CB00015B/2806